"I'd like you to meet my fiancé, Aaron Brody."

Charlie beamed at her speechless grandfather. She tried to present the picture of calm confidence, but inside her stomach lurched. What now?

Edward glanced at her bare ring finger, leveled his pointed glare at Aaron and demanded, "Is that true? Are you planning to marry my granddaughter?"

Locking gazes with Aaron, Charlie silently pleaded with him to back her up. His eyes matched the murky green of the gulf right before a storm, and were just as dangerous. Hopefully he was crazy enough to take the challenge.

"Why would Charlie lie about a thing like that?" Aaron asked without looking Edward's way. He slipped his arm around her shoulders and pulled her close.

Dear Reader,

I've always loved to travel, and my favorite destination is always a beach. But in all my travels, I've found no place on earth that matches the eclectic character of the Florida Keys. The Keys are more than a string of islands linked by more than seventy bridges. They offer a hodgepodge of open-air bars, hot sandy beaches and boats of every description. There are colorful locals, breathtaking sunsets and key lime pie. Romantic? You bet. But what if your job is creating romantic island vacations for other people and you never have time for love of your own? In fact, it's been so long since you've had a day off, you haven't even noticed anything is missing! Until one day he walks into your office. All muscled and tanned, his mischievous eyes twinkling as he flashes a roguish grin. You might consider doing something wild. Something crazy. Something completely out of character. But only as a last resort.

I'm so thrilled to be writing for Harlequin American Romance. Let me know if you enjoy escaping to the Keys with Aaron and Charlie in *Last Resort: Marriage.* I'd love to hear from you. You can contact me and find out about my upcoming books at www.pamelastone.net.

Wishing you sand between your toes, a salty breeze rustling the palms and a special someone to share it with.

Pamela Stone

Last Resort: Marriage
PAMELA STONE

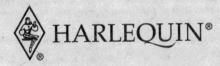

HARLEQUIN®

TORONTO • NEW YORK • LONDON
AMSTERDAM • PARIS • SYDNEY • HAMBURG
STOCKHOLM • ATHENS • TOKYO • MILAN • MADRID
PRAGUE • WARSAW • BUDAPEST • AUCKLAND

Recycling programs
for this product may
not exist in your area.

ISBN-13: 978-0-373-75271-3

LAST RESORT: MARRIAGE

www.eHarlequin.com

Printed in U.S.A.

ABOUT THE AUTHOR

Texas native Pamela Stone is an accounting graduate who spent more than twenty years in the technology field before publishing her first romance novel.

Pamela still resides in Texas with her childhood sweetheart and husband of—well, we won't mention how many years. In her spare time she enjoys traveling. From Hawaii to California to Florida to the Caribbean, if there's a beach, she's there. So not surprisingly, the majority of her stories are set on a beach. She also loves spending time with friends and family, but her laptop is never far from her fingertips for when that next inspiration strikes!

She insists that writing keeps her sane. Cheaper than a therapist and tons more fun.

I'd like to dedicate this book to my editor,
Johanna Raisanen, for taking a chance on me.
And to all my family and friends for believing in me.
And last but not least, to my critique partners,
Linda and Juliet. This dream wouldn't
have come true without you, ladies.

Chapter One

"After all, dear, you're not getting any younger," Charlotte Harrington's grandfather stated in a tone that made intelligent, self-assured adults quake in their shoes.

Not getting any younger? "Twenty-nine isn't exactly elderly."

"There's more to life than work."

Charlotte blinked. Since when had Edward Harrington thought about anything other than his precious chain of resorts?

"I only want to see you happy and settled with a husband and family. I want to hold my great-grandson before I die." He gestured to the man beside him. "Since you haven't found a suitable husband on this godforsaken island, I thought I'd help you out."

Perry Thurman held out both hands. "I miss you, darling."

Charlotte almost gagged. Perry wore his toothpaste smile and tailor-fit Armani with all the confidence of Edward's handpicked protégé. She drew a measure of satisfaction from the bump on his nose. Only the two of them knew the history of that little flaw.

Edward clapped Perry on the back. "Charlotte, Perry came to me and confessed that what happened between you two in college was entirely his fault. Give him another chance."

Her nails dug into her palms. Perry's sincerity might fool

some, but not her. There wasn't enough air in the room. She walked across her office and opened the shutters. *Think, Charlotte.* She glanced out at the beach where sunbathers baked on the clean white sand. She felt like the damsel in distress in one of her grandmother's romance novels. Perry fit the part of the despicable groom to perfection, but this was the twenty-first century and Charlotte wasn't buying into the plot.

She turned from the window to face Edward. "You, the man who lives and breathes work, are giving me advice about love?"

"There are a few things in my life I'd do differently. We all live with regrets."

Like being away on a business trip the day your wife died?

"At least hear me out before you reject my plan." Edward smiled that I-know-what's-best-for-you smile. "It's time you and Perry were back in Boston learning the ropes. Taking a more active role in Harrington's."

Charlotte caught her breath. Running Harrington's had always been her dream. Five years ago, she'd have jumped at a chance at a management position at the head office. But here in the Keys and away from her grandfather, she'd become accustomed to making her own decisions. She couldn't go back to working under Edward Harrington's thumb. And with Perry there, Boston sounded more like a prison sentence than a dream.

"Perry's done a phenomenal job with the Monte Carlo resort."

Typically, Edward seemed more interested in Perry's professional credentials than his husband potential. So much for the new family-first Edward Harrington. Begrudgingly Charlotte had to admit that Perry's profit margin was the highest in the chain. So why had he given up the prestige of running the Monte Carlo resort? His idea or Edward's?

"But what about this resort?" she protested. "I've turned Marathon Key into one of the most elegant, profitable resorts in South Florida." She glanced at the gold-framed diplomas, certificates and hotel awards on the wall behind her desk. "I was helping run it even before Daddy died."

"I already have several investors interested in taking this monstrosity off our hands."

"You're selling my hotel?" Marathon Key was all she had left of her father.

Edward glanced around. "It's the oldest resort in the chain. Nobody pays prime rates to come to the Keys nowadays when it's just as easy to hop a jet to the Mediterranean."

How quickly he dismissed everything she'd accomplished. Her chauvinist grandfather didn't have enough confidence in her to realize she could run her own hotel business without the help of a man.

"If you intend to sell Marathon anyway, then sell it to me. I can give you a hundred thousand down by tomorrow." It'd be tight, but some decent investments combined with her inheritance would cover it.

Edward clasped his hands together and smiled. "I'll do you one better. Marry Perry, move back to Boston and I'll sign Marathon over to you as a wedding present. You can play with it in your spare time. Bring your children down here for vacations."

So, the truth finally came out. He interpreted her hard work building up this resort as playing. Watching the two men exchange self-assured grins, she steamed. The conniving rats expected her to just fall in line with their conspiracy.

"You and Perry could make a good life together."

Perry eased behind her desk and took both her hands in his. "We were young. I was stupid. Any way you could find it in your heart to forgive me? Give me another chance?"

She pulled her hands out of his grasp and shot him a go-

to-hell look. Did he actually think she'd fall for his prepos-
terous act? She wasn't the naive coed she'd been six years
ago. Dimples and an expensive suit wouldn't fool her again.

Leaning close, he nuzzled her ear. "Don't be like this,
darling. We'll make a great team, both personally and pro-
fessionally. Just like we planned."

She flinched at his touch. The only thing Perry was interested in was getting to the top. He didn't care whom he had
to use, step on or obviously even marry to get there.

A quick tap on her office door drew her attention. Without
waiting for an invitation, the local Casanova strolled into the
room. "Hey, Charlie, we got a problem. My boat's on the
blink again."

Today was turning into a real winner.

"Charlie?" Edward sputtered. "You allow employees to
call you Charlie? How can you run a resort of this caliber
without respect for management?"

She bit her tongue to keep from snapping back. At least
they were in agreement about one thing. Only Aaron Brody
would enter her office unannounced and only Aaron called
her Charlie. The man had no concept of propriety or manners.
It was a miracle he managed to keep his charter business
afloat. Literally. This was the third time in two months he'd
had to cancel a tour because his boat wasn't running.

Ignoring her grandfather's comments, Aaron folded his
tanned arms across his chest and winked at Charlotte.

She did a double take. What was up with that? Did he
realize what he'd walked in on? She studied his face. She'd
never been able to decipher the strange workings of his mind.
Mr. Brody was a law unto himself. She'd long since given up
on him behaving properly.

The first time she'd seen Aaron Brody, he'd been
working on his boat. That situation hadn't changed much
over three years. The image of his sweaty tanned chest and

long legs dusted with sun-bleached hair was seared in her memory.

Cocky, independent Aaron would never get caught in a position like this. He'd probably tell Edward to go straight to hell.

As she studied him, an idea took form. Would Aaron go along with it? Either way, she wasn't about to lose this resort without a fight. But marrying Perry Thurman to keep it wasn't an option.

Trying not to act awkward, Charlotte sauntered up to Aaron and slipped her arm around his waist. She stared him straight in the eyes and smiled. "Aaron isn't an employee, Edward." Please let him follow her lead. She turned her head to watch the expression on her grandfather's face. "I'd like you to meet my fiancé, Aaron Brody."

Edward's jaw dropped.

She deliberately didn't introduce Perry as she beamed at her speechless grandfather. She tried to present the picture of calm confidence, but inside her stomach lurched. What now? Aaron surely thought she was a lunatic.

Edward glanced at her bare ring finger, leveled his pointed glare on Aaron, and demanded, "Is that true? Are you planning to marry my granddaughter?"

Locking gazes with Aaron, she silently pleaded with him to back her up. His eyes matched the murky green of the gulf right before a storm and were just as dangerous. She'd heard rumors of wild nights and wilder women. Hopefully he was crazy enough to take the challenge.

His body was a granite statue beneath her arm. Wiping her sweaty palm on the back of his shirt, she continued to hold his stare.

"Why would Charlie lie about a thing like that?" Aaron asked without looking Edward's way. He slipped his arm around her shoulders and pulled her close.

Before she had time to register relief, he bent his head, slid a seductive hand inside the collar of her blouse, and caressed her bare neck. He leaned close, rubbed the tip of his nose against hers, and covered her lips with his.

She felt every thump of her heart, but her lips parted, following his lead. His tongue slowly traced the shape of her mouth. She gazed into his eyes and her body temperature rose ten degrees. His mouth was warm and intimate, nibbling and sampling as if her lips were a delectable slice of key lime pie.

As quickly as he'd swept her into his arms, he loosened his hold. A corner of his mouth twitched and a mischievous twinkle lit his eyes. "You left before I woke up this morning. You know I don't like that."

Charlotte reminded herself to close her mouth. She couldn't think of an appropriate response.

Perry paced across the room. "You can't be serious about throwing your life away on this…this…"

She turned her back on him and flashed Aaron a grateful smile. "I have no intention of throwing my life away." Hopefully this "engagement" would buy her enough time to send Perry packing.

Edward ran his gaze over Charlotte before focusing on Aaron. "Is that the way you dress for work?"

She glanced at Aaron's dirty khaki shorts and road-stripe-yellow T-shirt. His sneakers sported holes and engine grease stained his shirt and nails. Tufts of sun-streaked brown hair stuck out from under a battered khaki baseball cap. Typical dress for the Keys, but not her grandfather's idea of proper business attire.

Aaron shrugged and pointed to the faded green words, *Brody's Charters,* stenciled on the front of his shirt. "You got a problem with free advertising?" The two men never broke eye contact. "This is the Keys, pal. Not Boston."

"So, when's the wedding? Should I postpone my flight?"

She couldn't move. She should have expected Edward to call her bluff. She squeezed Aaron's waist. "We aren't planning a big ceremony. Spring break is about to hit. Maybe after that we'll go to a JP."

Edward frowned. "A justice of the peace?"

"Charlotte, please don't do this." Perry sounded truly pained.

She took a breath and pretended Perry wasn't in the room. Not too difficult with Aaron massaging the back of her neck.

He rubbed his stubbled chin with his other hand and eyed Edward. "You know, Charlie, since your grandfather's in town, maybe my pal Johnny could marry us on his boat. He's a captain. We could get married as early as say... tomorrow."

Tomorrow? Her throat tightened. What was he doing? Did he think she was actually going to *marry* him?

Aaron flashed an innocent smile. "What do you say, Charlie?"

She felt like a swimmer trapped in a pool of circling male sharks. She offered her grandfather what she hoped was a pleasant smile. "Aaron and I need to talk. Could you give us a minute?"

She took Edward's arm and escorted him to the door. "Why don't you and Perry wait for us in the restaurant? Order lunch and we'll join you shortly."

Edward continued to watch Aaron.

Perry widened his eyes as if he were a parent instructing a child. "Don't let this guy rush you into something you'll regret."

She ignored him and pushed them out of her office.

The minute the door clicked shut she swiveled to face Aaron. "What are you up to?"

"Just playing along, sweetheart," he drawled, staring at her legs.

Smoothing her skirt, she stepped behind her desk. "I only

want to make my grandfather think we're engaged. The idea here is *not* to marry anyone. You just have to pretend."

"The hell I will! Your grandfather's not stupid. He wants you married or you're going to lose this place. Right?"

She swallowed. Edward hadn't exactly threatened that, but he always had an agenda. As, apparently, did Aaron. He was acting too sure of himself, too in control. "Were you eavesdropping?"

He quirked one eyebrow, but didn't deny her accusation. His sneakers squeaked across the polished wood floor as he sauntered over to pick up a crystal paperweight off her desk.

"What do you want, Mr. Brody?"

He put the paperweight down and propped one khaki-covered hip on the corner of her imported, mahogany desk. "Same thing you do. To save my business."

"I'm not following."

He dug a crumpled pack of Camels and a red disposable lighter out of the pocket of his shorts and lit a cigarette.

Charlotte fanned her hand in front of her face. "Don't smoke in here."

He paused with the cigarette midway to his mouth and then took a long drag before pinching the fire out between his fingers and flicking it into her empty metal trash can.

"A hundred grand should get me back on the water in style." Studying the smoke ring floating to the ceiling, he didn't glance her way.

"You *were* eavesdropping. Don't try to con me."

"Careful. You'll hurt my feelings." One eyebrow arched. "Look, you need a husband to pacify the old man and save your hotel. I've got a boat that needs a major overhaul and my funds are tapped out. We need each other or we'll both be out of business."

She narrowed her eyes. "A hundred thousand dollars? You're insane. I don't need you that bad."

"Yeah, you do. You marry that self-centered slick and Granddaddy will still be yanking your chain. Percy will lick that old man's wing tips until he keels over. Your grandfather will probably even put the resort in Percy's name." He sat up straight and did a realistic impression of Edward. "Isn't proper for a business to be in a woman's name. The man runs things." He turned and flashed an enigmatic grin. "But hey? You'll be too busy popping out little Percys to have time to run a hotel, anyway."

"Don't be a wise guy," she hissed. "And his name is Perry." Interesting the way Aaron had pegged Perry in thirty seconds flat. Whereas her usually astute grandfather seemed to believe the guy had feelings for anything other than his bank account. Edward had substituted the brown-nosing smooth-talker for the son he'd lost. Perry excelled in every aspect where her father had fallen short. Advanced degree in hotel management, professional appearance, and above all, a willingness to dedicate every waking minute to the Harrington empire. Perry hadn't been born a Harrington, but it was almost as if he'd been vaccinated with Edward's DNA.

Aaron grinned. "Think about it. We stay married a few months. I keep out of your hotel business and put my boat back in shape. Grandfather backs off. We get a quiet divorce and everybody's happy. Beautiful plan."

"Ten thousand for a pretend engagement."

"Come on, Charlie." He shook his head. "Short of marrying Percy, I'm your best shot at ever owning this place."

"I'll pay Edward the hundred thousand as a down payment and buy the resort. I don't have to marry either of you."

"Think of it this way. The resort is worth what, a hundred times that? You'll be paying on the loan for years. And as long as you're single, your grandfather will be riding your case about getting married and having a family. Pacify the old man. Marry me and he'll sign the hotel over to you."

"No. I'll figure out something," she said, although no immediate alternative came to mind.

He cocked an eyebrow. "Granddaddy's going to be disappointed when there's no nuptials tomorrow."

"What do you expect after your brash announcement?" she snapped. "I'll just have to explain." Somehow.

"You need me, Charlie."

She nodded toward the door. "Get out, Mr. Brody. I'm not marrying you or anyone else."

EDWARD STOOD AS SHE TOOK her seat across from him in the hotel restaurant. "Where's your fiancé?"

How could she tell him she'd lied about the engagement without making him so suspicious he'd never agree to sell her the resort? "Aaron had to arrange for someone to take his tour." She glanced around. "No Perc—Perry?"

"I told him to make himself scarce. Charlotte, are you certain about marrying this man? I've never heard you mention Aaron Brody until today."

"There are lots of things you don't know about me."

"As I'm sure there are things you don't know about your fiancé."

This was probably her best opening. "Look, Edward—"

"I don't trust this guy. He's seeing dollar signs."

"Perry's the one seeing dollar signs."

"Just because the man hurt your pride in college is no call to be snide. He's grown up. So should you." He leveled his gaze. "If I truly believed Aaron was in love with you, I'd be delighted. But…"

"You don't believe he could love me?" Maybe she wasn't the type men typically craved in their beds, but she wasn't exactly a dog, either.

"You're not thinking clearly. Love clouds a woman's judgment. I don't want you hurt and I have to protect my business. I've worked too damn hard to risk some fortune hunter taking you to the cleaners."

She twisted her napkin. If she didn't know her grandfather had her best interest at heart, she'd reach across the table and yank his red power tie until his face matched.

"Aaron isn't like that," she said, although not more than fifteen minutes ago, he'd tried to do exactly that.

Edward pushed his chair back and stood. "He is and I can prove it." With that parting shot, he turned and strode out of the restaurant.

AARON GLANCED UP FROM WORKING on his defunct engine and narrowed one eye as Edward Harrington boarded the *Free Wind*. One thing Aaron could say for the guy, he was better dressed than the typical clientele.

Harrington slid a leather checkbook from the breast pocket of his tailor-made jacket and flipped it open. "How much?"

Aaron grabbed a grease rag off his toolbox and wiped his hands as he stood. "Excuse me?"

"No games. How much to get you out of my granddaughter's life? What'll it take to make you disappear? Fifty thousand? A hundred?" Edward stared at him in disdain.

Nothing ever changed. He might as well be back on the streets of Miami with everyone who passed scowling at him as if he was slime that had washed in at high tide.

A flock of seagulls squawked overhead. Harrington glanced up and frowned as if he expected them to shut up on command. "A working-class man like yourself meets a woman of Charlotte's means and sees an opportunity to make a fortune." He scoffed at the greasy tools scattered across the deck and took a slender gold pen out of his pocket. "Well, she's not as vulnerable as you thought. You've got to deal with me. Two hundred thousand?"

Two hundred thousand?

Harrington nailed him with a stare, waiting for him to bite. Aaron pictured all the new equipment that much money could buy. Hell, he could get a new boat.

"Come on, Mr. Brody, every man has a price. Give it up. I'm not having my granddaughter taken by a two-bit crook."

Harrington's smug confidence burned his ass. Thought his fat bank account gave him the power to control the world. "Do you need a step-by-step diagram of where to stick that checkbook?"

Aaron had the pleasure of watching Edward's self-assured smirk fade as he replaced the checkbook in his pocket and strolled off the *Free Wind*.

He was going to hate himself in the morning. But hell, once Charlie told her grandfather she'd broken off the engagement the check would be about as worthless as his archaic engine anyway.

Chapter Two

"I may have been a bit rash in judging your fiancé," Edward admitted as he folded himself into the wing chair across from Charlotte's desk.

Her fingers stilled over her keyboard. "You're admitting you were wrong?"

"I wouldn't go that far." He held up one hand. "But I'm willing to give him a chance."

She shut down the spreadsheet she'd been staring at. What had transpired between him and Aaron?

"Let's face facts. To my knowledge, the only serious relationship you've ever had was with Perry. And look how you handled that."

Nibbling her lip, she told herself he didn't mean that quite how it sounded. He didn't know the full story. But then, she'd never actually leveled with him about Perry for fear of confirming his belief that women let emotions cloud their judgment.

"Getting along with people is not your forte."

A true enough fact, but it stung just the same. The man was a master at capitalizing on people's vulnerabilities. "Not my forte? I learned everything I know from you."

"Don't get upset. I'm trying to protect you."

She narrowed her eyes. "From what?"

"Yourself." He exhaled. "Now, you can marry your scuba diver—"

"I don't need your permission."

"No, you don't." Edward steepled his fingers. "But if you want this resort, you'll listen to my proposal."

She clenched her fists in her lap. As usual, everything had to be by Edward's rules.

"Aaron passed the first test, but I'm far from convinced that romance is his driving force. Still, I'm willing to give the marriage a chance. If, after say six months, I'm satisfied as to Mr. Brody's motives, I'll sign the Marathon resort over to you, like I promised. At least you'll have a means to support yourself."

Aaron had been right. He was her best shot at ever owning the hotel. But could she marry and pretend to be in love for six months? Could Aaron? It shouldn't be too difficult. They only had to put up a front when Edward was around, and he had twelve resorts demanding his time.

Edward cleared his throat. "Perry has agreed to stay on as your assistant manager. He'll report directly to me."

Her entire body tensed in outrage. She should have known he'd have a trump up his sleeve. "I don't need Perry."

"Take it or leave it." He folded his arms. "I have to look out for you and protect my business."

She bolted to her feet. "But I've been running this resort alone for almost five years."

"I'm not sure you're thinking with your brain at the moment," he said. "Of course, Aaron will sign a prenuptial."

"He already offered. I told him it wasn't necessary." If she was going to bluff, might as well pull out all the stops.

He looked at her as if she were some poor lovesick fool. "Oh, Charlotte!"

"I'm not as naive about men as you think. I know my

fiancé." She could handle Aaron Brody. On the other hand, she thought, remembering the kiss, maybe she *was* a poor lovesick fool.

CHARLOTTE STEPPED ON BOARD Aaron's boat, half hoping he wasn't there. Could she pull this off?

Easy to see why he needed the money. The *Free Wind* was a dilapidated fiberglass boat in desperate need of a face-lift. The hull had probably been white at one time, but had taken on more of a dirty yellow hue. The wood deck was warped.

She'd about decided the boat was deserted when she caught sight of him sitting behind a desk in a miniscule office.

The afternoon sun barely filtered through the salt-crusted window. He stood as she stepped through the door into the cramped, paneled office. "What did I do to rate two Harringtons in one day?"

She choked down her pride. "We'll have to draw up a pre-nuptial agreement."

Aaron frowned and crossed his arms over his chest.

"But ten thousand is my final offer." She adopted her don't-mess-with-me, business tone.

"Lady, I've been insulted enough for one afternoon. Take your money and do your husband shopping somewhere else."

Humiliation burned through her. She couldn't even buy a husband. Did he want her to beg? She shouldered her purse and turned to go.

But go where? Back to Edward and admit Aaron didn't want to marry her?

She straightened her shoulders and faced him. "You were right. You're my only viable option."

He leaned over, flattened his palms on his desk, and focused his sea-green eyes on her. "A hundred thousand, which I know you can get your hands on, deposited in an account in my name and I'll sign a prenup that says I walk away with my business and the money in my accounts." His jaw stiffened. "If it doesn't specify what I *do* get, I don't sign."

Charlotte let out her breath. She never thought she'd negotiate a marriage like a business contract. Who said she didn't know how to manage relationships?

"Let's make sure we understand each other. This is business." She leaned into his face. "We get married and Edward returns to Boston. In six months, providing we can convince him that a) we're blissfully in love and b) you're trustworthy, he'll sign the resort over to me. At that point, we file for divorce. And—" she paused for effect "—I have no intention of sharing your bed as part of the arrangement."

That announcement slowed him down a pace or two.

"And it won't kill you to take a couple months off from your playboy lifestyle."

"Playboy?" He looked genuinely surprised. "Just because I'm no damn monk? Don't tell me, you're saving yourself for marriage. Oh, wait, you don't want sex then, either."

Sarcasm dripped from his words. Okay, so sexuality wasn't her strong point, but still.

Aaron studied the top of his desk and took out his cigarettes. After a glance at her, he shoved the pack back in his pocket. "I'm not thrilled with sharing your bed, either, sweetheart, but you know as well as I do the old man won't believe this farce unless we share accommodations." He flashed a wicked grin. "Your place or mine, Charlie?"

The image of lying naked with this green-eyed macho maniac made her stop. She wasn't the quivering, breathless type and getting naked didn't figure into this.

He flashed another charming smile, and extended his hand. "Let me see your phone."

The man didn't even have a cell phone? She opened her purse and handed him the slim, silver device.

His grin was pure devilish amusement as he punched in a number. "And a good day to you, Sara. Is Johnny around?"

"What are you doing?" She narrowed her eyes.

He smoothed his knuckles slowly down her cheek. "I'm taking care of the church and the preacher for tomorrow, Charlie. Think you can handle the rest?"

AARON RAISED HIS SHOT GLASS and clinked it against Johnny's. "To a hundred grand," he repeated Johnny's toast and then chugged down the whiskey.

Raul Mendez, bartender and owner of the little waterfront, open-air dive, The Green Gecko, shook his head and scowled. "You really gonna go through with this?"

With three ex-wives, Raul looked a little sick at the thought.

"And she's not even going to sleep with you?" Raul sloshed more whiskey into his glass and guzzled the contents in one swig.

"That pretty much sums it up." Aaron grimaced, removed the cigarette dangling from the corner of his mouth, and stabbed it into an ashtray. "The sacrifices a man will make for his business." He reached across the polished wood bar, grabbed the bottle, and poured himself another shot. "By this time tomorrow night, I'll be a married man." He tossed back the golden glass of courage. "Sexless marriage and money to fix my boat. What more could a guy ask for?"

Johnny shook his head. "Let me get this straight. You've finally met a woman you don't want to bed and she's the one you've decided to marry?"

"You make me sound like some gigolo, for God's sake. The name of the game is money, and Charlotte Harrington has the money I need."

"You don't see anything wrong with marrying for money?" Raul asked.

"Women have been doing it for centuries. This is the new age. Equal rights and all that." Aaron stared at the bartender. "Need I remind you why Rosa left your ass?"

Raul rubbed one hand across his forehead. "Money."

"The root of all relationships, one way or another."

"Make sure your lawyer looks over that prenup before you sign it," Johnny advised. "From what I hear, Charlotte Harrington's a cold-blooded businesswoman. You know the type. All work and no play."

"Well, then maybe she won't bother me too much during this circus."

"*Sí*, she runs a tight ship, but Rosa says she's a good boss," Raul chimed in. "She says Senorita Harrington pays more than the other resorts and has good benefits." He grabbed a towel from behind the bar and wiped down the polished surface. "Rosa thinks Senorita Harrington is lonely." His eyes widened and he halted in midswipe. "*Dios!* Maybe she will enjoy having a man around and won't give you a divorce!"

"I don't have to worry about that." Aaron chuckled. "I'm not Miss Haughty Harrington's type. She's champagne and caviar. I'm pretty much beer and pretzels."

"I can picture you now bouncing a son on one knee and coddling a wee little daughter on the other," Johnny said.

Aaron winced. "You got the wrong guy. I have no intention of contributing my defective gene pool to any urchins. For now, I plan to fix the *Free Wind* and concentrate on building the most successful charter business in the Keys, courtesy of the Ice Queen." He raised his glass. "To weddings, my friends."

"To weddings," Johnny echoed.

Raul looked like he'd swallowed a rotten egg. "You gonna get frostbite."

Aaron paid his tab and made his way back to his boat on foot. The smoky little bar wasn't far from the slip where he docked the *Free Wind* and he needed some fresh air. Who was he kidding? He'd never even owned a car.

The night was balmy for early March, but a cool salty breeze rustled through the palm trees and fanned the hair off his neck.

God, he loved the Keys. Unspoiled by overdevelopment, far from Miami, a few exclusive resorts. Dressing for dinner meant putting on a shirt with buttons. He was his own boss. Nobody riding his case. Between the charter business and scuba instructing, he got by okay. At least he had until the past few months when his twenty-year-old engine had decided to play out. He could only wire it together for so long.

If Charlotte Harrington hadn't been so desperate, the business would've been history. He lit a cigarette and took a long drag. The kicker was he didn't know how to do anything else.

Aaron stooped and picked up a small conch shell. He'd never thought of Charlie sexually. The lady was a workaholic. That hotel of hers ran as smooth as a perfectly tuned pair of twin turbos, but she didn't seem to relax. He'd never heard anybody mention dating her or running into her at a club. Besides, her family owned a whole damn chain of hotels. She was so far above his reach the air she breathed was in a separate hemisphere.

He reared back his arm and lobbed the shell into the rolling Atlantic. The scorching summer afternoon he'd first met Ms. Harrington, she'd been wearing a navy suit with a silk blouse buttoned up to her chin. She'd stood out like a virgin in a whorehouse on the sweltering dock surrounded by people in shorts or swimsuits. How did she breathe in this tropical heat? But in three years, he'd never seen her look anything but calm, cool and collected.

Until this morning.

Grinding out his cigarette with his sneaker, he grinned. Charlie had squirmed when he'd put his hands on her today, as if his touch would soil her impeccable silk suit. Yet, her warm response to his kiss had been pretty damn willing.

What would cool, calm, collected Charlotte be like if she let her hair down? He'd never seen her thick dishwater-blond hair flowing free, not once. She always wore it twisted up in some French knot, or French braid, or French something. Man, her hair. It had to be long, and…

What was he thinking? He'd had too much to drink—and not near enough sex in the past few months.

Stepping across the gangplank onto the *Free Wind*, he climbed down the companionway to his cramped cuddy below deck and punched the switch on the radio.

He wasn't going to miss sleeping on this bucket of bolts. A soft bed instead of a lumpy berth, a real bathroom instead of a closet he had to back into just to sit on the head, and best of all, funds to fix the *Free Wind*.

The reality started to sink in.

Flopping down on the berth, he listened to the ropes clanging against the mast of the sailboat in the next slip and tried to forget that this time tomorrow he'd be married. He linked his fingers behind his neck. But all he could picture was Charlie, sprawled across satin sheets, those long legs wrapped around him.

Had he lost his ever-loving mind?

AARON FROWNED AT EDWARD Harrington's reflection in the department store mirror. The man had glued himself to his coattail like lint.

"A white tux?" Aaron shook his head, slipped out of the jacket, and tossed it back to the clerk. "Black."

The clerk scurried off and old man Harrington shrugged.

"Black is fine, if that's what makes you comfortable. Do you love my granddaughter?"

Forcing himself not to react, he focused on his reflection, combing his fingers through his freshly trimmed hair. "Look, Mr. Harrington. We rushed the wedding up so you could be here, but other than that, stay out of our business."

"My friends call me Edward."

"So does your granddaughter," Aaron commented.

"Yes, she does." Harrington tilted his head. "Charlotte's a smart woman. But, she needs a man who'll help her slow down and enjoy life."

"And you think Thurman would've done that?" Aaron scoffed in disbelief.

"Women need a family, a husband and children to love. A man to take care of them."

"Charlie can take care of herself." Aaron slipped into the elegant black jacket the clerk held up.

The last time he'd seen her, however, she'd been standing in the center of a horde of caterers and florists and looking as flustered as any real bride. Aaron grinned.

"Black suits you." Harrington straightened Aaron's jacket collar then selected a black bow tie from the two the clerk held out. "Pleated shirt and cuff links."

Why argue? He figured the guy had forgotten more about fashion than Aaron had ever known. He could be a model for some upper-crust magazine like *Senior GQ*. A poor-as-dirt kid on the streets of Miami, Aaron had been lucky to have secondhand jeans.

Harrington held the tie up to Aaron's white T-shirt then dropped his hand and pierced him with a menacing glare. "You do anything to hurt my granddaughter and I'll ruin you. You'll wish you'd never heard the name Harrington. You understand me?"

Aaron looked into his steel-gray eyes. How would he react

when, instead of producing a baby in nine months, they produced divorce papers? "I'll do everything in my power to make Charlie's dreams come true."

The man seemed to weigh his words. "I don't trust you. Something isn't on the level, but if you're the man Charlotte loves, I won't argue. Just keep in mind, I'll be watching every move you make."

He held his stare. "Yes, sir."

"And as the new assistant manager, Perry will be here to keep an eye on the business."

Aaron buttoned and then unbuttoned the jacket. No doubt, Perry was here to watch more than the business. The last thing they needed was Thurman snooping around.

He remained patient while they measured the tux for alterations. Before he could pay for the evening wear, Harrington handed the clerk a platinum card. Aaron started to object, but changed his mind. This whole charade was for the old man's benefit, anyway. Why shouldn't he shoulder the expense? Any man who'd force his own granddaughter to get married just to spawn an heir deserved whatever he got.

The clerk assured them the tux would be at the boat in forty-five minutes, altered, pressed and ready to go.

Aaron never failed to be amazed at the power of the almighty buck. "Great, I'll have fifteen minutes to dress and get to my wedding. Nothing like cutting things to the last minute."

"Do you have honeymoon plans?"

A pretend honeymoon wasn't part of the bargain. He had to get his boat running in two weeks or he'd have to cancel the tours he had booked for Spring Break. "Maybe we'll take a trip in the fall."

"A good marriage deserves a good start. A couple days shouldn't bankrupt either of you. Charlotte looks exhausted. Take time to relax and enjoy each other."

The old geezer actually seemed excited about the prospect

of Charlie getting laid. Did he think he could control their sex life, too? "Don't you have other children or grandchildren to worry about?"

Harrington huffed. "My only son—the self-centered playboy—married a starlet with a brain the size of a pea. Two of a kind. They were killed nine years ago in the Alps when they ran their snowmobile off a cliff."

"Charlie's parents?" Aaron winced at Harrington's nod, picturing how devastated self-reliant Charlotte probably was by the loss of her parents. "She must have been what, nineteen or twenty?"

"You two don't talk much, do you?" Harrington asked.

"Hasn't exactly been high on the priority list."

The old man pursed his lips. "Don, Charlotte's older brother, was in California at the time, studying acting. Like his mother in more ways than I care to discuss." Edward took a breath. "And then there's Charlotte."

"And then there's Charlotte," Aaron repeated. "There is Charlotte."

Chapter Three

Charlotte's head throbbed. Things were happening too fast. How could her entire life turn upside-down in thirty-six hours?

The reflection in the pink marble-framed mirror was that of a stranger. Soft curls teased her cheek. She shifted from one satin stiletto to the other and tried to stand still as the hairdresser fussed with the placement of tiny flowers in her hair. She fingered her grandmother's pearls. Today they felt more like a noose than a treasured family heirloom.

She'd never made use of the spa at the resort for more than an occasional massage, yet today Edward had pushed her into the shell-pink suites where her body had been massaged, waxed, buffed and conditioned. Her nails were French-tipped and the girl had painted a tiny white flower on her big toe. Subtle highlights streaked her freshly trimmed and curled hair. The artistically applied makeup put the two-minute blush and mascara she smeared on each morning to shame.

Edward had instructed Rosa, the woman who ran the resort boutique, to pick out a special outfit for the occasion. Rosa had been born with a rare gift for guessing a customer's size, taste and credit limit in the span of twenty seconds. Always attentive to details, she'd included an array of accessories, right down to a lacy blue garter.

Charlotte felt like Cinderella. All this feminine pampering would have made her mother proud.

Still, it seemed senseless for a pretend wedding. Okay, so the wedding was real, but the marriage was temporary.

To satisfy the old saying, she had a blue garter, a new dress and the heirloom pearls she'd inherited after her grandmother died. Charlotte closed her eyes. Did a groom count as something borrowed?

She just wanted to get this dog and pony show over with. Focus on the goal. If they could pull this off, in six months Edward would sign the resort over to her, Aaron would be history, and she could put this insane charade behind her.

Charlotte blinked at her reflection. Who was this chic woman staring back? She was getting married in... She glanced at her Gucci watch and gulped. "I'm late."

She smoothed her white linen tea-length gown, waved Rosa and the fretting hairdresser away, and hurried across the manicured lawn.

A lavish reception filled the Hibiscus Ballroom. Charlotte's personal attorney had Aaron's signature on the prenuptial agreement and the bank had approved the loan. Her stomach cramped. The payments on a hundred thousand dollars would put a sizeable crimp in her investment portfolio.

Palm trees swayed in the tropical breeze as Edward strolled down the sidewalk, looped his arm through hers, and whispered, "The most beautiful bride since your grandmother walked down the aisle fifty years ago. She'd be so proud. She worried that you wouldn't take time for a family."

Tears sprang to Charlotte's eyes.

She squeezed his arm. How could she love someone so much and want to strangle him at the same time? As much as she hated his ability to manipulate her, there wasn't a soul on earth who loved her except her grandfather. No matter how foolhardy his plan, his intentions were irreproachable.

They moved toward a small yacht that had sailed up to the resort dock an hour ago. It sported bright aquamarine trim and flew billowing flags. A dubious-looking captain in a flashy uniform stood at the helm amidst a forest of bright tropical flowers.

Bile rose in her throat.

You can do this. Just one foot in front of the other. The next time her feet touched this grass, she'd be a married woman. Married to Aaron Brody. She froze.

She hadn't eaten all day. Maybe she could faint and save herself from this self-inflicted lunacy. Except she'd never fainted, not once in her entire life, so the chances of that feminine ploy saving her from this fiasco seemed remote.

A resort wedding created excitement, but today's crowd seemed unusually enthusiastic. Guests stopped to smile and applaud as she passed. Aaron's friends and a handful of her employees waved from the deck. Strange time to realize she didn't have any friends, only business acquaintances.

Charlotte had always clung to the idea that if she ever did marry, it would be to a man she loved. A fat brown pelican taunted her from the corner post of the dock. So much for her one girlish fantasy. Clutching her grandfather's arm, she took a tentative step onto the yacht. A step away from her safe world. A step toward her new life as a deceiver.

The bridal march began. Her eyes searched out Aaron standing at the front of the boat. She let out a relieved breath. He'd actually shown up.

It took a minute to recognize him. He looked elegant in a formal black tux. Like a gentleman—suave, calm, almost eager. A flicker of surprise crossed his face before the charming smile returned. His eyes smoldered as she walked down the short aisle.

Aaron swallowed a lump in his throat as he watched Charlie approach. *My God, she's regal.* She radiated class from her upswept hair to the tip of her white sandals. Tall and slender, back straight as a soldier, head held proud, and wearing a flimsy white dress that rustled and clung to her curves as she glided toward him.

Tempting cleavage peeked out above the square neckline. Her arms were bare. Too bad the dress covered so much of her legs.

A few wispy strands of dark blond hair curled down her back and at her temples. Tiny white flowers cupped one side of her face in a gentle caress. She looked beautiful. Scared to death, but beautiful.

He crooked his arm and her grandfather placed her small hand on his forearm. Covering her slender fingers, he leaned close. "Slow and easy, Charlie."

Barely listening to Johnny's words as the ceremony progressed, he tamped down an unexpected surge of panic. He was getting—he swallowed—married. Married to a sophisticated heiress.

She had a wall full of diplomas and he hadn't finished high school. He tugged at his constricting collar, reminding himself of the papers he'd signed today. He sure as hell hoped that lawyer of hers had been on the level when he'd explained the agreement, but Charlie would have turned gray at the altar waiting for him to muddle through all those legal terms.

A hundred thousand dollars, Brody.

Johnny cleared his throat and Aaron realized everyone was staring at him, waiting for him to speak. Charlie focused straight ahead, but her manicured fingernails dug into his arm.

"I do."

The sound of released breaths, a few feminine sighs, and then Johnny recited some gibberish about rings being the symbol of eternity never broken.

Aaron took the ring out of his jacket pocket and slipped it

onto Charlie's finger. "It was my mother's." Why had he told her that?

She frowned at the cheap, tarnished band. Had she expected him to drop a bundle on a diamond?

"You may kiss your bride."

Placing one hand at the small of her back, he slid his other around her shoulders. Her eyes were huge as they stared up at him. They were the most incredible shade of brown. Dark and rich like the first cup of morning coffee, a shade shy of black. Whether it was the apprehension in her expression or her racing heart, holding her was like holding a captive bird. He wasn't sure if that was what turned him on, but something did. And she was his wife. For a few months, anyway.

He blinked and diverted his attention to her full lips. Pouting lips that turned down at the corners, waiting for him to take possession. His mouth closed over hers, gentle at first. The tip of his tongue teased her glossy lips apart.

Her body melted, becoming soft and pliant. He was amazed how small her waist was before his hands slid lower to pull her close. That frigid professional aura hid an exceptionally feminine body. Even her scent was an intoxicating fusion of self-assurance and vulnerability.

"Mmm," she whispered.

That faint murmur made his brain fuzzy. He lost track of time acquainting himself with the phenomenon that was his wife. Her fingers curled around his neck and her tongue ventured out to meet his.

Charlie's active participation in what started out as a simple kiss caught him off guard.

"Ladies and gentlemen, may I present Mr. and Mrs. Brody."

Aaron drew away from her mouth and took her hand. Cheers went up. Flower petals rained from the sky like a soft summer shower, blanketing the deck of the yacht in bright, fragrant color.

He looked at Charlie and winked.

They led their guests along the rambling sidewalk, across a narrow bridge that spanned the pool, and into the ballroom.

Mounds of delicacies adorned white linen-covered tables. Soft jazz filtered through the air from a band hidden away in the corner.

He put his arm around her waist as old man Harrington directed them to form a receiving line. Her expression hadn't changed since she'd plastered on the China doll smile when Johnny pronounced them husband and wife.

Typical of the Keys, people took their time stopping to chat and congratulate them. She fidgeted and twisted her new ring. He hadn't expected cool, calm, in-control Charlotte Harrington to get so uptight carrying out her calculated scheme.

He flagged down a waiter, snagged a glass of champagne, and offered it to his wife. His wife. "Take a sip. It's hot in here."

"I'm not thirsty."

He took a drink and held the glass to her lips. "It'll calm your wedding nerves."

Taking the glass, she scowled. "It is warm."

Aaron nodded at a passing waiter. "Could you see about cranking the air conditioner up a notch or two?"

"Yes, sir, right away."

Rosa and Raul were the last to make their way through the line. Rosa kissed first the bride then Aaron's cheek.

Raul's smile sparked pure devilish enjoyment as he shook Aaron's hand and leaned close. "Your wife is *muy elegante.*"

His friend was betting he wouldn't be able to keep his hands off her. He was careful that only Raul saw his obscene hand gesture. "Yes, she is."

Raul slipped his arm around Rosa, as if they'd never divorced, and strolled away. Would he and Charlie be friends after their divorce? Aaron took his bride's hand and raised his voice. "Let's get this party rocking." He nodded to the band and squeezed her hand. "May I have the pleasure of the first dance, Mrs. Brody?"

She hesitated. Would she actually turn him down?

"Come to me, beautiful lady."

She came into his arms stiff and unsmiling, but into his arms all the same.

"Don't overdo it," she warned, before turning to grace the room with her plastic smile.

He led her onto the empty dance floor. The lights dimmed and it only took a second to recognize the band's mellow rendition of "Strangers in the Night." He had to laugh at the appropriateness. Had Charlotte picked it? More than likely Johnny or Raul had put them up to it.

Their bodies meshed from chest to knee, but her steps remained stilted. "Relax, sweetheart."

"Call me sweetheart one more time and I'll go dance with Edward."

"He's talking to Percy." He considered Perry Thurman. "Not going to dance with my competition tonight, are you?"

"He was never anyone's competition. And besides, who I'm interested in isn't your concern."

Aaron slowed the steps to a sway and placed his hand on her hip, moving her with him. Other couples joined them on the dance floor and he held Charlie close. He could act the part of the adoring groom as well as the next guy. "Trust me. You show interest in anyone except me during this marriage, I'll make it my business. Making a fool of me wasn't part of the bargain."

"Oh, and you're going to stay celibate for the next six months?" Her eyebrows drew together and she eased out of his arms. "We should mingle with our guests." She grabbed a flute of champagne from a passing waiter and left him alone in the center of dancing couples.

Charlie gulped down the gold liquid as Perry moved in her direction. He touched her shoulder and without hesitation, she set her glass down and moved into the slime-bag's arms.

Aaron willed his fist to unclench.

He hadn't counted on Thurman breathing down their necks. He narrowed his eyes as Thurman's hand snaked up Charlie's side and his thumb rubbed the underside of her breast. Before Aaron could react, she took Don Juan's hand and placed it back on her waist. Okay, he couldn't very well stop her from dancing with the snake, but he didn't have to stand here and watch.

The last brilliant shades of sunset were fading from the sky when Aaron stepped outside. One smoke and a couple minutes to get his head straight, then he'd go back in and decide whether to deck Thurman or drag his bride out of his clutches. He lit a cigarette and leaned against the building. What had possessed him to agree to this?

As he took a drag and watched a kid on the beach feeding a flock of seagulls, he caught a glimpse of someone stepping onto the deck. He remained in the shadows and watched old man Harrington stop and take a couple of deep breaths. Edward pressed a hand to his chest, leaned against the rail, and dug something out of his pocket. The man looked pale as he tilted his head back and placed a pill in his mouth.

Should he ask if Harrington needed help or would that embarrass him? He waited until the older man was breathing easier before stepping out of the shadows. "Nice evening."

Harrington straightened and glanced casually over the ocean as if he hadn't just been clutching his chest. "Why aren't you inside with your bride?"

Holding up his cigarette, Aaron shrugged. "Just needed fresh air and a quick smoke."

"How do you exist in this humidity?"

A fine sheen of sweat covered the guy's ashen face. Taking

another drag, Aaron snubbed his cigarette out in a concrete ashtray. "I could use a drink. How about you?"

"Something cold does sound good."

"Thought I'd try the punch." He stood back and allowed Edward to precede him inside. "Somebody has to drink it."

Aaron handed Harrington a glass of pink punch and spotted Charlie standing beside a leafy palm. Before he could make his way across the room, Thurman appeared at her side, removed the glass from her hand, and guided her onto the dance floor. That made twice.

As Perry slid his arm around her waist, Charlotte noticed Aaron standing beside a table of caviar. She tried to focus on her dance partner and ignore the threatening glower on her husband's face.

Aaron Brody was legally her husband. She missed a step at the realization. Was he serious about demanding fidelity? Was he planning to "cleave only unto her"? Right! And the colorful tropical sun would set in the east tomorrow.

She couldn't complain about Perry's dancing, but the hand slithering down her back was another matter. He gently squeezed her hip. "You look wonderful tonight."

She grabbed his hand and guided it back to her waist, grinding her heel into his foot. "Don't start this."

He moved his foot back. "I've never loved another woman like I love you. I always thought…" Perry's breath stirred her hair and his tone sounded wistful, but all she felt was disgust.

Why the sudden interest after six years? Perry didn't do anything without a self-serving motive.

Edward tapped Perry's shoulder and she gratefully moved into her grandfather's arms.

Edward scrutinized her face, as if her debauchery was tattooed on her forehead. "Are you happy?"

Smiling took a concerted effort. "Of course."

He patted her back. "You look a bit nervous."

"You know me. I worry about everything. As fast as we threw this together, I keep thinking I've forgotten something."

"Everything you do is done to perfection."

Tears stung her eyes, and that made twice today. Her grandparents had taken care of her most of her life. Even before her parents died, she and Don had lived with them. Her mother and father had always been jetting off to a party at some villa or mountain resort.

He pressed her face against his shoulder. "Promise that if that groom of yours hurts you in any way, you'll let me know."

"Aaron would never hurt me." If he did, she wouldn't need Edward's help. She'd kill him herself.

"Well, I'll have to take your word for that. I just hope you know more about him than the size of his…"

"Edward!"

He spun her around. "I wasn't born yesterday, my dear."

Charlotte tried to relax and enjoy the reception, but every time she looked up, Aaron was whisking some other woman around the dance floor. He had all the right moves. Probably from all those bars he frequented. When he wasn't dancing, he was drinking with his buddies.

She turned and found Perry at the other end of the table watching her watch Aaron. He sidled up to Edward and she shuddered at what he was undoubtedly whispering in the older man's ear.

If she and Aaron intended to fool anyone, they needed to appear to enjoy each other's company.

She gritted her teeth and pushed through the crowd of men gathered around her husband. "Hi, darling. Come dance with me." She grinned at the group of laughing, half-drunk males. "Sorry, fellows, but I'm stealing my groom."

Aaron's arm slid around her waist as if it was the most natural position in the world, holding her close as he delivered the punch line of the joke he'd been telling. His hand dropped lower to caress her backside.

Resisting the urge to yank his hand away, she put her arm around his waist and tugged him away from his rowdy friends.

She placed her other arm around his neck, leaned close, and waltzed him onto the dance floor. "You aren't very convincing as the adoring groom."

Aaron rubbed his nose against hers and spoke into her mouth. "Then try this. Stay away from Percy or you'll find out how well I play the role of jealous husband."

"You have the nerve to worry about Percy? I mean Perry. You've danced with every woman in the room."

"If you were dancing with different men, I wouldn't mind. But how does it look that you've danced with Percy three times?"

He was counting? "And I'll dance with him again, if I want."

Aaron spun her in his arms and kissed her hard on the mouth. "Go ahead. I'm not too high-class to make a scene. You're mine, sweetheart. At least for the next few months."

Her temper wanted to fight, but her common sense warned her not to argue in front of the guests. "I don't belong to you or anybody else." Backing away, she tugged him toward the table where the wedding cake waited. "Shall we cut the cake, darling?"

The photographer snapped pictures as Aaron placed his hand over hers on the knife and they cut the first slice out of the towering white-and-pink creation. She smelled the alcohol on his breath, but at least he didn't mush the cake in her face.

Her relief was short-lived however, when to everyone's delight, he licked a crumb from the corner of her mouth. Her face heated as the room erupted into applause.

Then guests toasted them to everything from good luck to advice on how to maintain a long and fruitful marriage. She tried to keep from spitting champagne when the inebriated ship's captain toasted to a wild and passionate wedding bed.

Aaron didn't seem to mind the fellow's bad taste. He held up his glass and downed the contents. Every time she'd looked at him tonight, he'd been drinking.

Rosa set her glass down and handed Charlotte the bouquet. "Time to offer us single women a chance."

That sounded painless enough. She smiled, took the bridal bouquet, and waited for the women to gather. Rosa stood in the center, flanked by a couple other women who worked at the resort and a stunning Caribbean beauty. Even Zelda, Charlotte's latest assistant, joined in. Fifteen or more eager women battled for positions.

"Everybody ready?" she asked before turning her back. "Here goes." She tossed the bouquet to the chorus of excited squeals. She turned to find the Caribbean beauty clutching the bouquet to her breast like a treasure, but it wasn't her young escort who caught the girl's eye. It was Aaron.

Charlotte frowned, but before she had a chance to dwell on that, one of the men shoved Aaron toward her. "Your turn, my friend. Guys get their shot at the garter."

She gulped and shook her head. "I don't think—"

Aaron knelt down on one knee and rubbed the back of her ankle, flashing a devilish grin. "Can't disappoint the gentlemen, now can we, Charlie?"

His hand scorched through her stockings as he cupped the back of her knee. The other hand placed her foot on his bent leg. She held her breath and stared as he eased her skirt up her thigh and gently stroked upward in a reverent caress until he reached the lacy garter. Her skin burned as his fingers skimmed her inner thigh. She sucked air into her lungs.

Aaron slid the garter slowly down her thigh, over her knee,

and along her calf while she watched, mesmerized. He stretched the garter over her shoe and caressed the back of her leg as he softly kissed her knee.

"Incredible legs," he whispered, placing her foot back on the floor and glancing up into her face.

She diverted her eyes, refusing to react. Yet, her traitorous body responded too readily. Her stomach fluttered and she felt flushed and jittery. The imprint of his hands still seared her leg. Damn Aaron Brody!

Chapter Four

Was she drunk? Charlotte brushed sticky tendrils of hair off her neck as she and Aaron wound their way to her clapboard bungalow. Her eyes refused to focus. She had consumed more alcohol tonight than during her entire college tenure.

It was past 2:00 a.m. but that didn't stop Edward and Perry from chaperoning them to the door.

She didn't miss the folded check Edward discreetly pressed into Aaron's palm as they shook hands. "Just a little wedding present."

Aaron unfolded the check and glanced down. His lips tightened and he shoved it back into her grandfather's hand. "I can't accept this."

"You're family now. There's no reason you shouldn't accept it."

Aaron's jaw muscle ticked. "But—"

"Good night." Edward slid the check into Aaron's jacket pocket and stepped back.

Perry shoved his hands into the pockets of his slacks and rocked on his heels. "Well, Brody, I should say congratulations. Charlotte's made her choice, better man and all that." The veiled threat in his eyes wasn't lost on Charlotte.

"No problem, Percy." Aaron scooped Charlotte into his

arms, opened his mouth over hers, and sucked every ounce of air from her lungs. All she could breathe was Aaron. He broke the kiss and squeezed her bottom. "Now, if you'll excuse us, it's our honeymoon."

With that, he swung her through the door and kicked it shut behind them, leaving Edward and Perry on the porch. But Aaron was still fondling her derriere.

She squirmed. "Show's over. You can put me down."

He released her, sliding her body down the length of his and running his hands along her sides. Stopping at her breasts, he growled low in his throat and moved his hands to the front, rubbing his thumbs over her nipples.

A raw ache shot from her breasts to the juncture of her thighs. Embarrassed by her body's betrayal, she knocked his hands away. "Don't do that!"

He chuckled and turned to lock the door. "The flesh is willing, but the spirit's weak," he misquoted under his breath.

There was only enough light in the room to make out his smug smile, but she itched to slap it off his face.

His hand covered hers as she reached for the light switch. "No lights, sweetheart."

This sweetheart thing was wearing thin. "So I should just stand here in the dark and let you fondle me?"

"They're going to watch this place like vultures the next few minutes. If we turn on lights they'll know which room we're in."

His nonromantic, logic-based request chafed. "Well, we should close the shutters then, shouldn't we?" She turned toward the nearest window and flipped the slats down. The inky darkness engulfed them like an intoxicating cloud.

She heard Aaron's erratic breathing behind her as his hands tugged at her loose chignon. The pins pinged as they landed on the hardwood floor.

He plunged his fingers into her hair and murmured, "I knew it would be long and silky."

Fighting for control, she tugged her hair out of his grasp and stepped around him. "I'll get linens for the sofa."

Aaron caught her arm to slow her down and fingered the flowers that miraculously still clung to the tendrils of hair around her face. "You look stunning tonight." He began a slow seduction of her mouth, angling her head to penetrate deeper and rubbing his rock-hard length against her stomach.

Her head tilted into his palm, but her eyes remained open, leery, watching him. He tasted of champagne and wedding cake, a heady combination.

Long-dormant impulses caught fire, but she fought to maintain her decorum as his lips enticed hers to participate in his seductive game. The tip of his tongue tickled the inside of her top lip. She closed her eyes and reveled in the sensation. Aaron Brody knew how to kiss. Plenty of practice, from all accounts.

This was nuts. After Perry's betrayal, she'd promised herself never to allow anyone to use her again. Aaron had married her for one purpose—money. He wasn't even attracted to her.

She squeezed her arms between them and pushed, fighting his weight and will. "We agreed. No sex."

He grabbed her hand and placed it on his hard shaft, pushing into her palm. "I never agreed to no sex. That was your idea." He nibbled his way down her neck.

Charlotte shivered as he pulsed beneath her palm. It had been so long. And if she dared to be honest with herself, she'd thought about Aaron Brody's toned body quite often over the past three years. But she knew little or nothing about this man. And what she did know, she wasn't sure she even liked.

She snatched her hand away. "Aaron."

"Shh," he whispered, planting a trail of feverish, wet kisses across her shoulder. "It's our wedding night, Charlie."

His body was paradise, hard and ready to fulfill the fantasies he'd fueled that first day she'd seen him working on his boat in nothing but those stupid shorts.

Charlotte took a step back, but Aaron countered with one forward, dragging the back of his rough knuckles across her cheek in a feather-soft caress.

He took another step forward and she backed away. His palm turned and cradled her cheek as his tongue mated with hers, kissing her deep and hard, warm and wet, promising exquisite ecstasy.

What was she doing? She must be drunker than he was. It was dangerous to even think these thoughts. Husband or not, she hardly knew him. Yet with a few practiced kisses and gropes, he'd managed to turn her brain to mush. Forcing her legs to move, she took another step back from his sexual heat, but her back hit the wall.

Aaron leaned in, captured her right breast, and deepened the kiss. In pure panic, she ducked under his arm and wriggled free.

He groaned, resting his forehead against the wall. "Charlie."

The room was too dark to read his expression as he pushed off the wall and turned toward her, but it didn't take a genius to read his mind.

"I'm not doing this." She stepped into the bathroom, closed the door, and leaned against its protective barrier.

She'd take bets that in high school Aaron Brody had been every father's nightmare.

Flipping on the light, she reached behind her neck and unclasped her grandmother's pearls. Staring at her reflection, she wondered how she'd compare to his host of lovers. Too skinny? Too flat? Too brainy? She'd heard it all. Then, in college, when she'd finally trusted Perry and opened her heart to him, he'd betrayed her. He'd had sex with some brainless bimbo and they'd laughed at her.

But Aaron hadn't laughed, a small voice whispered. Yeah, but he was too drunk to care, her practical side countered.

Easing the door open, she followed a trail of clothes and found Aaron lying across the bed flat on his stomach, illuminated by stripes of moonlight filtering through the bedroom shutters. Stunned by his nakedness, all she could do was stare wide-eyed at the exquisite specimen of raw masculinity in her bed.

Lord have mercy, his body was perfect. His arms raised above his head emphasized the muscled physique of a man who daily earned his living swimming and hauling heavy scuba gear. Muscled back, narrow hips, tight little butt.

Her breath caught. The events of the past two days were surreal. She hadn't set out to marry Aaron Brody, it had just sort of happened.

Burrowing deeper into her thick terry-cloth robe, she forced herself to approach the bed. "Aaron," she whispered. "What have we done?"

No response.

She touched his shoulder. "Aaron?"

He didn't move. His only answer was a soft, rhythmic snore.

Her groom was sound asleep.

AARON OPENED ONE EYE and groaned as the light stabbed a knife of pain through his temples. An army of construction workers ran jackhammers inside his head. Closing his eyes, he willed the wrecking crew to take a break.

He rolled over and squinted, but his stomach churned. This time he caught a glimpse of a tall bedpost, with a canopy frame. He steeled himself for the pain and opened his eyes.

The walls were white, with a couple of bright photographs of flowers. The furniture looked expensive, too contemporary for his taste, white like the rest of the room. A huge white ceiling fan rotated slowly above the bed.

Where— He bolted up and grabbed his throbbing head,

suddenly remembering. Charlotte Harrington! Correction—Charlotte Brody.

The past forty-eight hours slapped him in the face, but he could only remember bits and pieces after he and Charlie arrived at the bungalow.

He was in Charlie's bed, but where was she?

Coffee. He needed hot, black coffee. He lifted the sheet and stumbled naked out of the bedroom, in search of the kitchen.

He stopped when he saw his wife—his wife!—curled up on the sofa. She looked innocent and fragile, sleep-flushed, her lips slightly parted. Nothing like the hard-assed woman the resort employees called the Ice Queen.

Vague remembrances of last night flashed through his pounding head as he squatted in front of this stranger he'd married. Every time Thurman had danced with Charlie, Aaron had sloshed down another beer. He couldn't figure out why her dancing with that jackass had bothered him so much.

He lifted the crocheted afghan and took a long look. Gray knit sleep shorts cupped the curve of her hips, leaving her long legs exposed for his pleasure. The tiny lavender crop top didn't quite meet the waistband of the shorts. Not exactly a wedding night negligee, but sexy in a Charlie sort of way. Her dark nipples puckered beneath the thin, soft fabric, rising and falling as she slept.

One thing that came back to him with stark clarity from the night before was how perfectly those breasts fit his hands. Her body had enough curves to keep things interesting. A couple strands of blond hair cascaded over her shoulder and between her breasts.

Unable to resist, he rubbed the silky tresses between his thumb and forefinger and brought them to his nose. Coconut.

He stared at her legs. Long, luscious legs. He could imagine them wrapped around his hips as he—

Dropping the afghan across her lower body, he slogged through the foggy muck in his mind.

He had a vague recollection of making out with her. Of her body in his arms.

She'd seemed as turned on as he had, but then she'd bolted like some schoolgirl who'd just found herself alone with a man for the first time. Guess the heiress didn't want to lower herself to make love with a scuba guide. He didn't delude himself about why he was here. He was good enough to help save her business, but not to warm her bed.

Fine. She didn't want to have sex with him during this ridiculous marriage. He had plenty to keep him busy. His boat required major repairs. His books were a mess and he had to find somebody to print up a first-class brochure.

But Mrs. Brody wasn't getting off the hook that easy. They still had to fool her grandfather.

Using the lock of hair for a feather, he trailed it around her nipple then upward until it tickled the end of her cute little nose.

She sniffed and swatted at it as if it was a pesky fly.

Pausing long enough for her to relax, he repeated the procedure.

Her nose wrinkled and her hand swiped it away, coming into contact with his.

Charlie's eyes flew open and she turned to stare. "Ohh," she groaned, massaging her temples. "My head."

"Good morning, wife."

She scrunched her eyes closed.

He wanted to laugh, but he didn't think he could stand the pain. "You know, the locals have a special cure for hangovers."

"They do?" She peered through squinted eyes.

He leaned close until their lips touched. "It's called—" he covered her mouth and kissed her until she began to actively participate in the game "—*una copa rica de café!* But you'll have to make your own coffee. I have a business to run." He pushed away and stood up, flashed her a wicked grin, and headed to the bathroom.

CHARLOTTE STOPPED ON THE WAY to her office to put her grandmother's pearls back in the hotel safe, dragging in after ten to find Perry Thurman looking comfortable and relaxed behind her desk.

"What are you doing in my office?"

He eased her lap drawer closed. "Just helping out. We assumed you'd take a few days off to…well, you know."

"How dare you search my desk? And don't just assume you can use my office." She raised her eyebrows in a haughty look she'd learned from her grandfather.

"Whatever you say, boss." Perry stood and shoved a legal-sized sheet of paper in her direction. "But at some point we need to discuss this."

Oh, God! Had he found her copy of the prenuptial?

She rubbed the back of her neck, stepped closer, and glanced at the paper. It wasn't the prenup. Feeling her heart start to beat again, she narrowed her eyes at Perry. "What is it?"

"You pay your front desk staff ten percent more than market. Could be why this resort isn't turning the profit it should."

Every word out of his mouth infuriated her. She called on her depleting reserve of calm professionalism. "Don't question my management decisions."

Perry remained behind her desk, wearing an innocent smile.

She moved into position on the other side of her chair and crossed her arms.

He didn't budge. "Charlotte, please tell me you didn't marry Brody just to hang on to the resort. I feel responsible. If I hadn't hurt you so badly before, maybe you wouldn't have rushed into this marriage so quickly."

Swallowing her disgust, she stared him straight in the eyes. "I didn't rush into anything. I've been in love with Aaron for three years," she lied.

"You've been having an affair with this guy that long and never mentioned him to Edward?" He laughed. "What can someone of your upbringing have in common with a guy like him?"

"You couldn't possibly understand." Being rejected by a woman he didn't want for a man he considered rungs beneath him had to be a blow to Perry's sizable ego. She walked around the desk, opened the door, and gestured him out. "Anything else?"

He swallowed, shook his head, and left her in blissful silence.

She shut the door behind him and leaned against it to regain her composure. Six months of this?

Perry was a poor loser. And as shrewd as he was unscrupulous. He might fool everyone else with this caring pretense, but not her. He had something up his sleeve and whatever it was, it had more to do with his quest for power than his heart.

She buzzed Zelda and asked her to bring in coffee. Although, the way her head pounded, she wasn't sure coffee was going to be enough today.

Remembering Aaron's "cure" of black coffee, she nearly choked. He'd seemed completely at ease with his nudity this morning. Closing her eyes, she tried to imagine herself traipsing around her bungalow in the buff. Not in this lifetime.

Blinking Aaron out of her mind, she grabbed her purse and rummaged for her bottle of aspirin. Finally, she gave up and dumped the contents on the desk. What was that? A check made out to Aaron from her grandfather in the sum of twenty-five thousand dollars. On the notation line it simply said, *Best Wishes.*

She folded the check and stashed it in her wallet to deal

with another day. Aaron had every legal right to cash it, but he'd left it in her purse?

Popping the top off the bottle, she shook two tablets into her hand and laid them aside, waiting on the coffee.

What had Perry really been doing in her office? If he got wind of the prenuptial or the loan she'd taken out, the game was over.

She shuffled through her lap drawer, and then flipped through the caddy where Zelda left the mail.

"Maybe I lucked out this time." When the documents arrived, she'd store them in her safe deposit box and have all the locks changed on the office. She drummed her fingers on the desk. The snake had already charmed the keys out of either Edward or Zelda.

The savory aroma of steaming coffee followed Zelda into the office. Bless the girl's efficiency.

"Have a seat, Zelda."

"Yes, ma'am." Zelda tugged at her miniskirt and wiggled into the wing chair.

Charlotte noted her tight blouse and lime green skirt and made a note to discuss proper office attire—tomorrow.

Zelda had only been in the position two weeks. She had to be better than the last girl who quit to stay home with her baby. Baby or not, how could a woman trust a man enough to be solely dependent on him? Charlotte would never give any man that much control.

"You're aware that Mr. Thurman is the new assistant manager?"

"Oh, yes, ma'am. Everybody knows. He's very nice."

Nice my ass. The man was just waiting for a chance to vault to the top of the Harrington empire. "Did you give Mr. Thurman the keys to my office?" she asked, trying not to sound accusing.

Zelda fidgeted. "No, ma'am. Mr. Thurman said you'd be out for a few days. I unlocked the door. I didn't give him the key."

Leaning forward, Charlotte took a deep breath and tried to squelch her anger. "I count on your unquestionable loyalty. Whatever information you learn in this position is to be kept confidential."

The girl continued to nod, tears swamping her big brown eyes. "Absolutely, Ms. Harrington. Uh, I mean Mrs. Brody."

"Why don't you call me Charlotte?" She couldn't stomach being called Mrs. Brody just yet.

"Okay, Charlotte." She twisted a lock of spiked hair at her temple. "I just thought. I mean with him being assistant manager. It won't happen again, I swear."

Diplomacy was not Charlotte's strong suit, but she tried to instill a sense of teamwork. The last thing she needed was Zelda spreading the rumor that the manager didn't trust the assistant manager. "It's okay, but don't let anyone into this office again without my permission. And, Zelda, do you need a copy of the dress code?"

Zelda's scolded puppy expression made Charlotte feel like a tyrant. When everything settled down, she'd take another one of those online classes and brush up on her people skills. But with Perry and Edward looking over her shoulder and this ridiculous marriage to contend with, it would have to wait.

She had no more than hung up from calling a locksmith when Aaron burst in. "Did you know your secretary's crying?" He pointed a thumb toward the door.

She couldn't answer for a moment as she pictured him the last time she'd seen him, wearing nothing but his naked glory. She shuffled the papers on her desk. "You obviously had a purpose for barging in here other than to worry over my secretary."

"Yeah. Where the hell's my money?"

She rubbed her temples. Did his head ache as bad as hers? "What are you talking about?"

He braced his hands on her desk. "I ordered a new engine

for the boat and they won't ship until it's paid in full." His eyes pierced hers. "But the bank says there aren't enough funds in my account."

She picked up the phone and tried not to let his demanding tone get under her skin. "They're probably holding the check for twenty-four hours because of the large sum."

While she listened to the bank representative, her gaze followed Aaron's tight butt as he paced back and forth across the room.

"Thank you." She hung up and tried not to sound patronizing. "The funds will be available tomorrow morning."

He didn't even say thank you. "Time's money. You, of all people, should understand that. Every day I'm off the water is costing me," he tossed over his shoulder as he opened the door.

Perry was standing at Zelda's desk.

Charlotte breathed in. Her plan didn't have a chance if she and her husband didn't at least try to get along. "Aaron, what would you like to do for dinner tonight?"

He turned and narrowed his eyes, his voice oozing with sarcasm. "I don't know, Charlie. What did you have in mind?"

After last night, she didn't want to spend the evening alone in the bungalow. Too much temptation. "Let's try that new restaurant on Big Pine Key. Check out the competition."

She pulled out the brochure and dialed the number for reservations.

He stepped back in and closed the door. Without a glance at the brochure, he strolled over and broke the phone connection. He lowered his voice. "I think it'd be more convincing if we stayed home tonight. Give us a chance to devise a game plan."

Good point. They needed to look like happy newlyweds. After all, they'd only been married one day. "Okay, I'll call and have dinner delivered."

Aaron turned on his heel and left without another word. She

watched him pause at Zelda's desk. Even he wouldn't flirt with his wife's secretary, would he? She closed the door and growled in frustration. Controlling her resort with Perry lurking about paled in comparison to trying to control her new husband.

Chapter Five

Charlotte walked into her bungalow and stopped short at the sight of Aaron parked in front of the television. He held a beer bottle in one hand and the TV remote in the other. His bare feet were propped on her glass coffee table and he appeared immersed in a local show about the reef.

"Why don't you get comfortable?" He took a swig of beer. "Thought we'd eat on the patio."

The man was invading her life. Yet, outside was less intimate than in. "Fine."

While Charlotte changed clothes, she heard the waiter arrive with the meal. She followed the aroma of dinner through the kitchen and out the back door. Funny, she'd lived here five years and could count on one hand the number of times she'd eaten out on the patio.

The sun was setting and the breeze had lost the afternoon heat. She sat across from Aaron and watched as he lit candles. The sun streaks in his brown hair weren't as pronounced since he'd had it cut for the wedding. It had a slight curl from the humidity, adding a rakish flair.

"I hope you like smoked salmon. I wasn't sure what to order," she said, making an attempt at small talk.

He filled her wineglass. "I'll pretty much eat anything that doesn't eat me first."

Charlotte took a sip. "Where did you grow up?" She really knew nothing about the man she'd married.

"Miami."

She waited until the silence became awkward, hoping he might elaborate. Obviously, he wasn't in a talkative mood. "Do you have family?"

"My mom died when I was sixteen."

Charlotte fingered the inexpensive gold band he'd placed on her hand the night before. "This was her wedding ring?"

He nodded.

"I'm touched that you'd let me wear it. I'll make sure you get it back after the—" She left the sentence unfinished, uncomfortable mentioning divorce when they'd been married only twenty-four hours.

"She never married. Bought it in a pawnshop to keep the lowlifes at bay while she cleaned hotel rooms."

"Never married?"

His green eyes penetrated hers, challenging her to disapprove. "Nope."

"I guess money was tight," she offered, not sure what else to say.

"We got by." He forked a bite of shrimp cocktail.

"Have you ever been married?" she asked.

"No."

Where was all that charm the women of Marathon Key raved about? Guess they weren't referring to his social skills, but more to his… "Engaged?"

"Once. She dumped me." Aaron topped off their wine and focused on his dinner, effectively ending the conversation.

Before she had time to finish half her salmon, he pushed his empty plate back and lit a cigarette.

"I cannot understand why anybody would contaminate their body with that filthy habit."

Aaron took a puff. "Enjoyment. You do know the definition of the word?"

She reached across the table and eased the cigarette from between his lips. "I don't enjoy smelling secondhand smoke." She ground the cigarette out. "Consideration for others. You do know the definition of that, don't you?"

His eyes narrowed, but he didn't light another cigarette. "Well geez, Charlie, it's eight-thirty. You've eliminated smoking and sex from the agenda. What do we do now?"

Looking for any excuse to keep them out of the bungalow, she stood. "How about a walk on the beach? We're suppo~?d to be seen together, looking blissful and in love."

"Fill me in on the script," he said, falling in step beside her as she headed toward the lapping surf.

The moon floated just above the horizon, casting a silvery ribbon across the water. "We should make sure Perry sees us together at least once a day. Edward, too, as long as he's on the island," she explained. "When he feels comfortable, he'll return to Boston."

Aaron kicked at the edge of the surf and picked up a small piece of driftwood. "First we have to convince him that we're in love. Wouldn't hurt if you kissed me occasionally. Hey, I wouldn't even mind if you pinched my ass."

"I'm trembling in anticipation." She blocked out the temptation. "And it's always so pleasant to kiss cigarette breath."

Undaunted, he slipped his arm around her waist and patted her bottom. "I'll keep that in mind."

Her body tensed.

He leaned in closer. "You're going to have to quit flinching every time I touch you."

"I'll try. But lose the act. Nobody's watching."

His arm dropped to his side. "No problem, sweetheart."

Why did she feel like he'd dashed ice water in her face? Even though she'd rebuffed him, she'd thought…hoped? *Get over it, Charlotte.* She'd learned years ago that men didn't get hot over flat-chested, brainy women.

"I'm sorry about your mom. She must have been awfully young."

"Thirty-two. We sort of raised each other." Aaron flung the driftwood boomerang-style back into the rolling waves. "It was a long time ago and she was sick and not too thrilled with life, anyway."

"She was only thirty-two and didn't want to live?" Charlotte couldn't comprehend not fighting for life, especially with the responsibility of a son to care for.

His jaw set and he stared directly into her eyes. "Well, princess, not all of us are born with a silver spoon. Sometimes life just plain stinks."

"What did she die of?"

"Doesn't matter. She's dead."

Her blood boiled, but before she could respond, he pulled her into his arms and his lips began a tender caress down her neck and shoulder. Both hands cupped her bottom pressing her close.

She reached behind her and grabbed his hands. "What are you doing?"

"Thurman's coming down the beach." He clasped both her wrists in his hands and locked her against him. His lips scorched a path up her neck, the underside of her chin, the corner of her mouth, then covered her lips in a kiss that was anything but ambivalent.

His tongue rushed to mate with hers, darting in and out, enticing hers to participate in the sensuous ritual. Charlotte reluctantly joined in the game, acting her role of the enamored wife.

Aaron's callused hands roved beneath her blouse.

Her body grew warm and moist. She forgot this was all for show and reveled in the sensuous movement of his lips. Leaning her head back, she ground her hips into his. The waves lapped against the shore, the sound hypnotic as it lulled her senses. His kiss seemed to be in pace with the tide, ebbing and flowing with an age-old rhythm.

"Hello, Charlotte. Brody."

Perry's Boston drawl dragged her back to reality. Backing away from Aaron's seductive kiss, she touched the tip of her tongue to her lips.

Aaron enjoyed the dazed look on Charlie's face as her tongue slipped out to touch her kiss-softened lip. Was this the same cold resort manager he thought he knew? She didn't appear to be in any frame of mind to deal with Thurman at the moment. "Evening, Percy."

"You two look cozy out here on a public beach."

Keeping one hand on her ass, Aaron made sure she remained plastered against him. "We were, actually. Did you need something?"

"No." Perry shrugged. "Just out for an evening stroll."

Right below Charlie's bungalow? "Well, don't let us break your stride."

Perry shot him a menacing look and headed back in the direction of the resort.

"Jackass." Tomorrow he'd snoop around and see if he could find out what Thurman was up to.

Charlotte wiggled out of his arms. "He's trying to prove our marriage is a farce."

"I'd say we put on a good show." He dogged her heels as she stomped off toward the bungalow.

She didn't look as pleased as he'd have expected. Slamming into the bungalow, she stopped in the kitchen. "Aaron, you're taking this sexual act too far. I'll try to relax and be more responsive when we're in public, but keep your hands off my butt."

"Why?" He considered her request. "We're attracted to each other. What's wrong with enjoying the game? You need sex as much as I do."

"I don't need sex. I need a decoy until I can get Edward out of my hair."

"You're lying." Charlie had turned to hot molten lava on the beach, not to mention her reaction the night before. Would she ever admit she enjoyed his touch? "Want me to demonstrate?"

If her rich-coffee eyes could shoot daggers, he'd be dead. "Stop right there. We aren't going through this every night. Business partners don't have sex. I'll make up the sofa."

"Married couples do and I'm sleeping in our bed." He headed for the bathroom. "You can sleep wherever you want."

The dark side of his personality, the one his mother had referred to as the son of the devil, was itching for a shot at seducing the ice heiress.

Charlotte narrowed her eyes as Aaron disappeared into the bathroom. No way was she going to sleep on the sofa while he enjoyed the luxury of her king-sized bed.

Aaron walked out, a towel knotted precariously low on his hips. The purely sexual impact slammed into her stomach. Damp hair tasseled down his forehead and she had the urge to wrap a curl around her finger. He had the kind of rugged handsomeness that made women melt. Tan, slightly stocky and biceps men like Perry would kill for.

In frustration, she grabbed a nightgown and headed for the only room in the house that provided a measure of privacy.

The scents of soap and aftershave permeated the steamy bathroom. She couldn't even see her reflection in the mirror. The man was invading every nook and cranny of her space. With him living here, there wasn't the tiniest corner of the house that she could call her own.

By the time she reentered the bedroom, the only sign of Aaron was the damp towel crumpled on the closet floor. Where had he gone? She huffed. She wouldn't put it past him to hook up with one of his girlfriends. Aaron Brody didn't seem the type to go without sex for long. Or he could be smoking and drinking himself into an early grave with his obnoxious buddies. What did she care?

Her only concern was that Edward or Perry might see him leave, or worse, run into him somewhere. Well, at least she could rule out the latter. Unlikely that either of them would be caught dead in the type of establishments her husband frequented.

She opened her underwear drawer and meticulously folded every single feminine garment until the drawer passed her most stringent inspection. That was one part of the house she was confident Mr. Aaron Brody wouldn't disturb.

What did she need with a sexy womanizer complicating her life? After all, Perry had been charming, too. Aaron, Perry, her father. All they wanted from women was a good time. Brains were optional.

AARON WALKED INTO THE Green Gecko and straddled a stool. He ignored Raul's I-told-you-so expression and drummed his fingers on the bar. "Whiskey."

The bartender poured a shot and set it on the bar with a thud. "Little chilly tonight, *sí?*"

"*Sí,*" he agreed, surveying the packed room.

Johnny was at a table attempting to pick up a blonde who'd wandered into their local little web. As she giggled off in the direction of the ladies' room, he sauntered over and took a seat next to Aaron. "Details, my friend. How was the honeymoon?"

Raul held up a hand and tried to silence Johnny. Aaron shrugged. "I told you guys I had no intention of bedding the ice heiress."

"Oh? So why the scowl?" Johnny asked.

Rosa sidled up behind Johnny and took the next stool. "The woman doesn't know how to take care of a man. You're going to have to teach her."

"Me?" Aaron smirked. "I tend to gravitate toward warmer climates."

She shook her head. "There are women who are born knowing how to enjoy men and women who aren't."

Aaron eased past Johnny and slipped his arm around Rosa. At least he could let his hair down with his friends. "So stop talking, darlin', and give me a demonstration."

"If I found myself married to a man with your skills, I wouldn't kick him out of bed." She raised one pencil-thin eyebrow and rubbed her heavy breasts against his chest.

Rosa would no more sleep with him than Charlie would, but her flirting helped soothe his wounded ego. It had been a long time since he'd known a woman as detached as his wife. "So you'd marry me and chain me to the bed?"

She tossed her head back and led him toward the dance floor. "Marriage, never. But if you played your cards right, I might consider the bed and chains."

When the dance ended, Raul handed him another whiskey. "So seriously, what's it like married to the hotel tycoon?"

"We have nothing in common. She wants to eat at that new place on Big Pine Key. Looks overpriced and stuffy. I probably couldn't even pronounce what's on the menu." Or read it. Aaron lit a cigarette and wished they'd change the subject.

Looking him up and down, Rosa narrowed her eyes. "You plan to wear that?"

"Not planning to go."

"Tsk, tsk, tsk. Aaron, you're a handsome man. Show that lonely wife of yours a good time. Come by the shop and I'll dress you up."

"No way. I'm not coming in there and risk having my wife know I need someone to dress me." He took a drag of his cigarette. God, it was stifling. Even with the open front of the bar and ancient ceiling fans, the salty breeze didn't offer much relief.

Raul leaned across the bar. "So you dress the part."

Johnny slapped him on the shoulder. "Besides, might get you into her bed."

"I don't want in her freakin' bed! I just want to fix the *Free Wind.*"

Rosa squeezed his arm and he didn't miss her winking at Raul. Once a couple had been married, they seemed to develop some secret code. Not likely that he and Charlie would be together long enough to develop any sort of domestic lingo.

WHEN CHARLOTTE ARRIVED AT the office at six-thirty, a large tour rushing to make an early morning flight had the checkout desk jammed. She made sure the bus was ready to take them to the airport and stepped behind the counter to help hurry the line along.

She'd woken this morning to find one hairy leg draped across hers and a hand cupping her breast. Aaron must have crawled into bed in the wee hours of the morning. Ignoring her body's reaction to the warmth of Aaron's breath on her neck, she'd eased out of bed. She was probably the only woman on the island who had slept with Aaron Brody and not *slept* with him.

As she tried to concentrate on assisting another customer, she listened to the tour director's complaint about the buffet breakfast not being ready at six o'clock as promised.

To her amazement, Perry strolled in and took the woman's hand. "Ms. Carmichael, I'm so sorry for the mix-up. We've deducted twenty percent from last night's lodging and complimentary donuts and coffee are on the van. We hope you won't hold this against us on your next visit to the island."

Ms. Carmichael glared at Charlotte and took Perry's hand. "I do appreciate your effort, Mr. Thurman."

Narrowing her eyes at Perry, Charlotte headed to her

office. She had to find someone to cover for the absent morning chef before the next wave of guests woke up.

Perry followed her into her office. "I called the lunch chef to fill in."

"Thanks." She let the receiver drop back into the cradle. "How did you know?"

"When I got here an hour ago, the guests were in chaos."

An uneasy feeling niggled at Charlotte. The Perry she knew in college had never signed up for a class if it started before 10:00 a.m.

AT ELEVEN FORTY-FIVE Charlotte walked out of the resort with no idea where she was headed. She never took lunch, but if that arrogant jerk said, "If you'd just…" one more time she was going to stuff him down the laundry chute.

Perry had infiltrated every aspect of her hotel and she couldn't even fire him. How could he have charmed his way into Edward's good graces without that shrewd old man seeing through him?

Easy. She'd given him a glowing recommendation. Perry's booming career with Harrington Resorts was entirely her fault. Chill bumps ran down her arms at her own naïveté.

She glanced up and realized she was approaching Aaron's boat. Seeing him step off the *Free Wind* and give Rosa a hug jarred her out of her musings. Her Rosa? The same Rosa who ran the resort boutique? The lady he'd danced with at least twice at the wedding reception?

Unable to stop herself, she followed them down the narrow street, trying to keep enough distance so she wouldn't be noticed. She paused in front of a bright turquoise souvenir shop. A faded wooden sidewalk sign squeaked in the breeze and touted pictures of seashells, sunglasses and flip-flops. Assorted tropical T-shirts hung on a rack by the door.

Rosa was at least ten years older than Aaron. He stopped

abruptly at the next shop and grinned at the display in the window before Rosa tugged him away. Charlotte dodged a bicyclist and waited until they ambled on. She raised an eyebrow at the red thong bikini-clad mannequin in the window.

The sound of clanking dishes and laughter filtered out of an open-air bar as she passed. Smoke hung heavy in the dim cave of a room, even though there was no wall on the sidewalk side of the bar. The light tropical breeze seemed to trap the smoke in rather than air it out. The wooden sign swinging overhead labeled it The Green Gecko. Rickety wooden stairs clung to the side of the clapboard building leading to an apartment perched over the top of the bar.

Rosa and Aaron entered a small shop. Charlotte remained outside, squinting to see through the salt-filmed glass. Rosa sorted through a rack of slacks and handed a pair to him along with a black shirt. He disappeared behind a curtain only to reappear wearing the outfit. Rosa ran her hands down the front of the shirt.

What was going on here? Why was he buying clothes? Was Rosa just helping him shop or was there more?

"Hmm?" Perry taunted from over her left shoulder.

She wanted to crawl in a hole and die. No! She wanted Perry to crawl in a hole and die. "He's shopping," she replied, grappling for a plausible explanation.

"Shopping? While his new wife waits on the sidewalk?" Perry noted her peeved expression. "Makes perfect sense."

"I'm meeting Aaron for lunch." Damn, how was this going to look?

"Take all the time you need. Edward and I have things covered." Perry smirked and strolled off down the street, hands in his pockets, whistling some stupid, perky tune she half recalled from nursery school.

Slinging her purse over her shoulder, she stomped back

toward work. She couldn't take much more of this nonsense. If she didn't figure out how to get rid of Perry 007 Thurman, this whole plan was going to crumble like a sandcastle at high tide.

By the time she walked back to the resort, Edward was poking around the front desk making the staff nervous. Given his reputation for being blunt, callous and unforgiving, all he had to do was show his face and people freaked out. He seemed to revel in their discomfort, claiming it separated the boys from the men.

"Hi, Edward. Buy me lunch."

He shook his head. "I've eaten. Do you put these clerks through the training curriculum before scheduling them on the desk? That girl's messed up the customer's check-in twice and she isn't done yet. Does she understand English? I'll have Perry to schedule them for a refresher course."

Perry? Taking his arm, she led him toward the dining room. "You're making her nervous. Join me while I have a salad."

Charlotte kept him occupied at the table long enough to give her front desk employees time to calm down. The waitress handled her job with professional courtesy. Too bad all her employees couldn't have the woman's self-assurance.

AARON STROLLED INTO CHARLOTTE'S office around three o'clock, hands in his pockets and staring at his sneakers.

She tilted her head and tried to figure out his mood. Did it have something to do with his shopping spree?

"I thought we might try that new restaurant tonight, if you're game?" he suggested.

"You're asking me to dinner?" The puzzle pieces fell into place. If she weren't so clueless about reading people, she might have fit them together sooner. When she'd asked him to dinner last night, he hadn't had anything to wear.

He shrugged. "Sure, why not? Need to keep up the pretense."

"I'll make reservations for eight o'clock, if that works for you?"

"Yeah, that's fine. Gotta go. They're pulling the boat out and putting it in dry dock this afternoon."

The day had been a disaster, but after Aaron left, she couldn't keep from smiling. He was making an effort. Dinner might be a good start. A little cooperation could go a long way toward making this nightmare bearable.

When Edward stuck his head in, it was already past five. "I just got a call from a Transworld tour director. He has a group in town at another resort. He's not satisfied with the accommodations and is eager to discuss future business."

She read his mind. There went dinner with Aaron.

"I told him Perry would be happy to discuss it over dinner. Just wanted you to be aware."

Perry? "No need for Perry. I'll take the tour director to dinner."

"Didn't want to interfere with your evening."

"Not a problem." Grimacing, she tried to squelch her disappointment. She told herself it wasn't so much that she was looking forward to spending an evening with Aaron, but rather that she hated the idea of spending it with a boring tour director.

Edward flashed a grin. "I'll add one more to the reservation. Seven-thirty. I'm sure you and Perry can handle things."

Charlotte called the Conch Fritter Restaurant, cancelled the reservation, and then rang the bungalow. No answer.

She ran home to freshen up and change before dinner. She'd stop by the dock on the way and let Aaron know about the change in plans.

When she opened the bungalow door, she found Aaron dripping wet, a fluffy pink towel slung low around his hips. Any other man would have the decency to not look so sinfully masculine wrapped in pastel pink.

"Hi."

Charlotte rubbed her forehead and tried not to watch the droplet of water trickle down his chest, circle his navel, and absorb into the snug towel. "Bad news. We have to postpone dinner. I've got to entertain a tour director tonight."

He didn't respond for a minute, simply stood there.

"No big deal. I'll catch dinner with the guys."

As good of an actor as he was, he could have pretended to be at least a little upset.

As LUCK WOULD HAVE IT, the tour director didn't know when to shut up, and Perry added to the situation by leading the conversation from one boring topic to the next. They talked about every golf course on the face of the earth, hole by hole. Charlotte was tired and ready to call it a night, but the men rambled on like long-lost buddies. Perry had the guy eating out of his hand.

She and Perry finally saw the tour director into a cab and walked back into the lobby. He slipped his arm around her shoulder and gave her a squeeze. "We make a good team, you and I. Imagine what we could do running Harrington's."

Before she realized his intention, he leaned down and covered her mouth with his. "Nice evening, Charlotte. Like old times."

She jerked away, but he grabbed for her arm.

Aaron stepped out of the shadows and grasped Perry's lapels. "Touch my wife again and I'll feed your skinny ass to the sharks."

Chapter Six

Charlotte grabbed her purse, flipped off the light switch, and locked her office door behind them. "What's with the jealous act? Don't you think you overreacted just a bit?"

"Overreacted?" Aaron led the way to the bungalow. "You break a date with me to spend the evening with Thurman and don't think I should act jealous? What kind of husband would I be?"

"Oh, come on, Aaron."

His jaw clenched, poised for an argument. "So I should stand around and just watch him kiss my wife? You are paying me to act like a husband."

She stomped across the grounds and up the walk of her bungalow. "For a hundred thousand dollars I expect you to act civil. I didn't overreact when I saw you and Rosa shopping together today, now did I?" Oops.

He tilted his head. "You were spying on me?"

"I wasn't spying. I just happened to be walking by that little shop." She dug her key out of her purse and jammed it into the bungalow's lock.

"You don't just happen to do anything. Every move you make is a calculated tactic. You were checking up on me."

She stormed in the door and pitched her purse on the coffee table. "And what were you doing at the hotel tonight if you weren't checking up on me?"

"You let that slime kiss you."

"I didn't let him do anything. And Rosa had her hands all over you when you were trying on those clothes!"

Aaron scratched his head and a grin teased the corner of his mouth. He took a step forward. "Come here, Charlie."

Instinctively, she stepped back.

Reaching out, he caressed his palm down her cheek. "Who's the jealous one?"

Unable to think straight, she couldn't come up with a plausible defense for this softer Aaron. "I guess I was, a little."

One hand slid to the small of her back, gentle as it urged her toward him. His sexy sea-green eyes stared into the depth of her soul as his mouth descended over hers. Protest faded. Never in her life had she experienced such a powerful, seductive kiss. His fingers skimmed over her face, exploring every feature as his lips and tongue did the same to her mouth. He tasted faintly of whiskey.

"Dinner tomorrow night. Don't stand me up." He gave her one last temperate kiss. "Good night, Charlie."

She stood mesmerized as he disappeared into the bedroom. She heard the mattress squeak beneath his weight, while she stood in the living room like a schoolgirl who'd just received her first kiss.

The last thing she'd expected was to be courted by her husband.

DINNER GOT OFF TO A PLEASANT start. Aaron ordered margaritas and Charlotte listened to his plans for the boat. For once he seemed to be in a congenial mood.

"What's a depth finder?" she asked.

"It shows the depth of the water and the shape of the

terrain." He grinned and used both hands to simulate the boat and the ocean floor.

Tonight she saw a glimpse of the charmer the women of Marathon Key knew and loved, even though she understood only about half of what he said.

"You can see schools of fish or shipwrecks."

In the middle of his explanation, Charlotte's cell phone chimed. She dug it out of her purse, irritated with the interruption.

Perry wanted to know if she'd checked the morning schedule and was sure they had enough help to cover the desk.

"Perry, it's fine. I'm at dinner. We'll talk tomorrow."

As their frozen margaritas arrived, Charlotte looked up and saw Edward strolling toward their table. Her stomach sank. She'd hoped to enjoy a quiet dinner with Aaron and get to know him. She wasn't up to putting on a show for her grandfather.

"Perry said you'd rushed out of the office. He heard you had reservations here. Always good to keep an eye on the competition. Mind if I join you?"

Perry had overheard they had reservations here? Right. He'd been snooping through her calendar. "Of course not. Have a seat."

"Aaron?" he asked, as if he cared what Aaron thought.

Aaron gestured toward the vacant chair. "Be our guest."

Edward's gaze raked Aaron's shirt. "Nice to see you cleaned up tonight, Brody."

To his credit, Aaron didn't respond. She loved the way he looked tonight, dressed in a pair of khaki Dockers and a black shirt.

She studied her menu. "They're a little pricey. I wonder who their chef is. I heard a rumor they stole Antonio from the Pirate's Den for some outrageous fee."

"Is he worth it?" Edward asked, studying the menu. "Any of the same entrées?"

"I'm having the fresh Florida lobster. If Antonio's the chef, I'll know." She closed her menu.

"What can a chef do to a lobster that you'd recognize?" Aaron asked. "You just drop them in boiling water."

She grinned. "Yes, but it's the seasonings you put in the water that bring out the flavor."

"I'm having a steak." He snapped his menu shut with hardly a glance.

Edward continued to scrutinize every entrée. "They're about ten percent higher than we are. I'll bet the food doesn't warrant the prices."

"Antonio's creations do. I've tried to lure him away before, but he refuses to be associated with a hotel. Says it has a negative connotation."

"What are conch fritters?" Edward asked.

Aaron looked bored with their shoptalk, but she preferred to keep Edward's mind occupied with something other than her marriage. The ploy didn't last.

"So, Charlotte, you've kept yourself buried in work. Planning on taking time off for a honeymoon?"

Aaron winked and placed his hand over hers on the table. "We're having our honeymoon, aren't we, sweetheart?"

She tried to divert the direction of the conversation. "Edward, I told you, it's different here in the Keys. Spring Break's starting."

"I didn't let your grandmother out of the house for a month after I finally slid that ring on her finger. Chuck was born before our first anniversary." He wiggled his eyebrows.

Charlotte cringed.

Aaron downed half his margarita and smirked. "Well, I suggested we take a few days off, but you know your grand-daughter—work, work, work."

She frowned at Aaron and tried to pull her hand free. He gave it a quick squeeze and then released it, only to slip his arm around her bare shoulders.

The corners of Edward's mouth turned down. "I'd just like to hold my great-grandson before I die."

"Edward, please. All in good time. You're not going to die anytime soon."

He hesitated a few seconds before pushing on. "Time could be shorter than you think. You turn thirty next year."

"We'll have a child when we're damn good and ready," Aaron said.

Edward's eyes widened.

Aaron took a drink and thumped his glass back on the table. "Don't you think it's a little strange that a man your age takes such a keen interest in his granddaughter's sex life?"

So much for congeniality. She couldn't decide how to glare at both Aaron and Edward at the same time. She kicked Aaron under the table. Baiting her grandfather wasn't in their best interest.

Edward stared Aaron down. "I would like some assurances that I'll hold my great-grandchild sometime in the near future."

"What do you want, play-by-play? Want to watch?" Aaron finished off his drink. "Maybe we should forget dinner and go at it right here on the table."

"Stop it! Both of you." Charlotte flashed first her grandfather then her husband a warning glare. "Enough!"

Aaron smirked. His expression clearly said, "He started it."

She narrowed her eyes at her dinner companions then turned and smiled at the waiter. Edward had always been outspoken, but this tactless conversation was beyond even his norm.

She steered the conversation back toward food. The meal was tense, but Edward didn't push the subject. Aaron remained quiet.

Charlotte kept the conversation going, while inside she seethed. She wanted to strangle them both.

NOT A WORD PASSED BETWEEN Charlotte and Aaron during the drive home from the restaurant. She slammed the door on her Volvo and stomped toward the bungalow. "Don't ever talk about me like that again. How dare you carry on such a conversation?"

Aaron pushed ahead of her. "I wasn't any more out of line than that dirty old man. Yell at him."

"You could exercise restraint, a little judgment."

"Me? Don't you get it? Harrington's no fool. He's playing us. He can tell we aren't lovers. You barely tolerate my company. Who do you think you're fooling, Charlie? Not that old codger. Not that asshole who's trying to get in your pants." He paused. "Your name may be Brody, but you're still acting like Charlotte Harrington."

She searched his face. His jaw was set, but there was a measure of hurt in his eyes. "You've got it wrong. This isn't about you."

"You're right. So why didn't you just marry Thurman?"

"I don't love Perry."

He didn't flinch. "What difference would it make? You don't love me, either. You sure as hell don't want me in your bed."

"I'm not going to sleep with someone who's bedded every female under forty this side of Miami."

"Is that what's chafing your ass?" Stuffing his hands into his pockets, he let out a deep sigh. "What are you holding out for, Charlie? A dream lover who's saved his virginity waiting for the right woman? He'll take one look at you and grovel at your feet in awesome wonder?"

She winced at the image and crossed her arms. "I'm not having this conversation with you."

He grabbed her wrists and raised her arms above her head,

then pressed her against the wall, molding himself to her. His calloused hands sparked fire along the inside of her arms. His mouth was hot and wet on hers. Her traitorous body heated and responded to his nearness.

There had to be some sin involved with lusting after someone you didn't really know, even if that someone happened to be your husband. She couldn't afford to be attracted. He was simply fulfilling their deal and looking for a little sexual release on the side. She hooked one foot around his ankle and spun him.

The air swooshed out of Aaron's lungs as his back slammed against the wall. One minute he'd been kissing Charlie and the next instant he couldn't breathe.

"Don't shove me around," she spat through clenched teeth. "Let's see how you like it."

"Actually, it's sort of a turn-on." God, she was a firebrand when she was steamed.

She pursed her lips. "You're impossible."

If she wanted to play physical, he could handle that. He'd discovered enough over the past few days about what turned her on to know it wasn't being wooed by a soft touch. She was too tough for that. Charlie needed a man who could hold his own.

He took his time, seducing her mouth until it became supple and submissive. Her tongue had already proven that it enjoyed tangling with his. He shoved her skirt high and plunged his hands beneath the fabric and up her thighs to cup her round bottom through the thin satin panties. He imagined them being some soft pastel color, but they could have been army-green for all he cared. They felt sexy as hell.

Her hand squeezed his ass. He waited until she started panting and made that little moan she always made when she got turned on. Then, easing back just far enough to speak, he challenged, "Know what, Charlie? If you ever find your rich, virgin Adonis, you're going to be disappointed. You're too hot for a white-collar wimp. You'll be paying me or somebody else for stud service."

He didn't move, just stood and waited for her to respond.

Confusion wrinkled her brow and she nibbled her bottom lip. "So we have sex. Is that the solution? You think that would solve our problems?"

"You excluded sex from the original agreement, remember? If you want stud service, that'll cost extra." He jerked his shirt over his head, tossed it on the chair, and strolled into the bedroom, unzipping his slacks.

"Aaron?"

He heard his name, but couldn't fight anymore. Charlotte Harrington might want a wimp, but Charlie Brody needed a man.

Sex with her would be…wow. The fact that she was either too naive to realize it or too stubborn to admit it didn't lessen the chemical combustion.

He shucked the dress slacks and yanked a pair of shorts and a T-shirt out of the drawer. He tugged on his clothes, shoved his feet into his flip-flops, and headed for the back door.

"Where are you going?"

She sounded like a pissed off wife. "To pull the engine in my boat."

"Tonight?" She looked at him as if he was a couple beers short of a six-pack.

"Why not?" He sure as hell wasn't getting anything else tonight.

Aaron slammed the door, lit a cigarette, and started toward his boat. Dammit! He needed a woman. And he wanted Charlie Brody.

She didn't have a clue. There was a look a woman had when she was sleeping with a guy. He couldn't explain it, but he could spot it from fifty yards. Charlie didn't have that look and her grandfather knew it.

Didn't matter how hot and bothered she got, Charlie pushed him away. But mention that her control-freak grandfather might guess they weren't lovers, and then she decides that they should have sex? What did she think he was, a gigolo?

And then there was Thurman. Charlie had paid Aaron rather than marry the guy. She claimed to detest him, yet she seemed more at ease with Perry than she obviously was with him.

Screw it! He didn't need this.

He climbed the ladder onto the boat, relieved to be away from that immaculate bungalow. The boat might be an old rusty tub, but it was preferable to battling with Charlie. He didn't have to wear uncomfortable clothes and go to pretentious restaurants. He didn't have to clean his fingernails or not smoke. They were his lungs and his money that paid for the damn cigarettes. If he wanted to smoke, he'd damn well smoke!

He was sitting on the edge of the engine compartment, up to his elbows in greasy engine parts, when he heard someone climb aboard. He looked up and frowned at his wife. "What do you want?"

Not a sound. She didn't even answer his question. Husband. Stud. Now she expected him to add mind reader to the list? What did the woman expect for a measly hundred grand?

He jerked on the ratchet and the bolt broke free. Anger was good. He'd been tugging on that bolt for five minutes.

Charlie turned off the radio in the middle of the Eagles singing about heartache tonight and her hand gripped his shoulder. He remained focused on the engine.

"Aaron, look at me."

He glanced over his shoulder. Her eyes were liquid, missing that professional self-control. Her hair was still knotted on top of her head, but tendrils had come loose and curled around her neck. The sundress she'd worn to dinner left her neck and shoulders exposed. But that wasn't the difference. It was her soft, confused expression.

"You're going to get greasy." He didn't really care, but he figured she did. He finished unscrewing the bolt he'd just popped loose and tossed it into an empty coffee can.

"Can you stop a minute and talk to me?"

He didn't want to talk. She'd made her feelings clear from the start and discussing their situation wouldn't change a thing. He was nothing to her except an insurance policy to keep her resort.

She didn't belong down here on the dock.

She didn't belong on this bucket with him.

Yet, she didn't look like she planned to leave until she had her say. He hoisted himself to his feet and grabbed a grease rag off the toolbox. "What do you want, Charlie?"

Shifting from one sandal-clad foot to the other, she nibbled her bottom lip. Should he be flattered by how nervous he made his wife? He kept quiet and let her wrestle with whatever was bothering her.

She stared him straight in the eye and spoke in that infuriating professional tone. "I think you're right. We're fighting this attraction too hard. I can't sleep for thinking about you. I don't understand what's happening between us."

Was she actually as dense as she acted? It appeared the whole man-woman concept was beyond her realm of comprehension. "I'm a man. You're a woman. Pretty simple stuff."

"So, we should just do it? Then we'd both feel more comfortable," she stated, nodding.

He glanced down at his greasy arms and hands. Even if

he'd been tempted by her emotionless invitation, her timing stunk. "Right now? Just like that?"

She twisted her wedding ring and stared at her sandals. She was incredibly sweet when she wasn't so sure of herself. He liked this vulnerable Charlie. He admired the nerve it took for her to come here.

"Yes, let's just do it. Come back to the bungalow and shower."

"No way, sweetheart. We play this one on my turf."

Chapter Seven

What had she done? She'd just asked Aaron for sex! Straight-out, asked for it. Her heart pounded. Charlotte opened the tiny refrigerator and found a bottle of water among the assortment of beers. She needed to keep her wits.

The boat rested high on blocks, like a stage, except there was no audience. The wharf was quiet, almost eerie.

She rolled the icy plastic bottle across her heated forehead. If she rationalized her resolution according to logic rather than caving to lust, it would work. 1) Aaron was an attractive man with healthy male needs. 2) They both wanted sex. 3) Sex was a natural, biological act. 4) As he said, it would add certain legitimacy to the relationship and convince Edward.

Her decision was based on pure logic. That look of hurt vulnerability she'd glimpsed in her tough, macho husband had nothing to do with it.

She twisted the top off the water and took a drink as Aaron stepped back on deck. She gulped. His damp skin glistened in the moonlight. His hair was slicked back, still wet from his shower, and he wore only a pair of khaki shorts. That's all. No shirt, no shoes, no jewelry. Like that first day he'd caught her attention, he was sizzling, irresistible sex appeal personified.

He walked over, set her water on the counter, and took her hand in his. "We'd have more privacy below deck."

Her nerve floundered. She wanted him, but sex would change the relationship. Was she prepared for that? Would she disappoint him? Would he expect sex every night? If he did, would that be such a terrible hardship?

Preceding him down the narrow steps, she fought to remain steadfast in her plan. She was in control. This was a conscious decision she'd made to take the relationship into the next phase and relieve some of the tension.

A streetlamp cast the only light through the small door and window. She couldn't believe Aaron had lived in this cramped little cabin. The whole place would fit inside her bedroom. Narrow galley, bathroom the size of a closet, and a bed that didn't look big enough for one adult, much less two. She turned and found him watching her appraise his home.

Silently, he stepped behind her and leaned around to nuzzle her neck. Tilting her head, she allowed him better access. His hands were firm as they closed around her waist, holding her steady. The combined fabric of her sundress and his shorts weren't enough to disguise the condition of his body as he pressed tight against her buttocks.

His hands caressed upward and began the tedious task of unbuttoning the front of her dress. She leaned back against his chest and tried to stay calm. His body was hard and so very masculine. There was no grasping to fondle her breasts or touch her skin as his hands continued methodically, button to button.

The night air chilled her breasts, then her belly. His hands moved lower and his palm pressed against her flesh as he struggled to free the buttons closest to her crotch. Her knees wobbled as he tugged the dress higher and continued to work the buttons free.

He released the last button and the dress hung loose. Aaron pushed her away, slipped his hands beneath the thin dress straps, and slid them down her arms, dropping the garment to the floor.

Charlotte tried not to whimper, standing frighteningly vulnerable in only her panties.

Pulling her back into place, his lips tickled her left ear as one hand covered her right breast. Her breathing hitched as he slid his other hand across her belly, down her abdomen, and inside her panties.

Breathe, Charlotte. Breathe, in and out.

He palmed her at first, rubbing and stimulating her senses. Could he feel the steam his feathery touch released? She didn't wait for him to tell her to open her legs. She didn't even consciously do it. They simply opened to his magic. His finger slipped inside her and began to slide in and out, slow and methodic, working her into a heated frenzy.

"Tell me what you want, Charlie," he whispered. "Let me make you feel good." His other hand left the warmth of her breast and pushed her panties down, granting his fingers easier admittance. His hand pumped faster. "Do you want to lie down on the bed?" Harder, his fingers kept up their ceaseless pulsating probing.

"You want to bend over the bed? Against the wall?" His tongue traced the curve of her ear before he leaned forward, turned her head, and kissed her full on the mouth. "You want it gentle? Rough? Talk to me."

Her mind reeled. She had a choice. She couldn't think beyond breathing and he wanted her to make a choice?

Spinning her around to face him, his free hand pushed down his shorts. She tried not to stare at his naked body, but she couldn't tear her eyes away.

Holding her hips, he dropped down on the edge of the bed and pulled her forward to straddle him. "Bend your knees and wrap them around me."

She did as instructed, her body on fire. "Oh," she panted,

not able to conjure up words. She'd never wanted to be with anyone like she wanted to be with Aaron. She'd never been in this position, straddling a man. She smoldered as he sucked one breast into his hot mouth, running his tongue around her nipple. Her body shuddered and she broke out in a sweat anticipating his next move.

"Aaron, are you here?" A feminine voice from somewhere far off interrupted Charlotte's euphoric haze.

One second she was in bliss, the next she found herself lifted away from his warmth and deposited on the bed.

"Grab the sheet, sweetheart. This'll just take a second."

He donned his shorts and climbed topside.

Charlotte didn't recognize the woman's husky voice, but she could only assume it was one of his ex-lovers, or current lovers. She had to get out of here.

She searched for her panties and dress. What had she been thinking coming here? This was a mistake. How could she have convinced herself that it made any kind of sense to have sex with the playboy of the Keys?

She was still fumbling with the buttons on the blasted dress when she met Aaron on the stairs.

"Where are you going?"

The man wasn't stupid. He should be able to figure it out. "Home."

"Why? She's gone."

Okay, so he was a moron. "Sorry, I changed my mind. I'm not going to become another notch on your scuba belt."

She started to move away, but he caught her arm. "How many women do you think I've slept with?"

"How should I know? Even that lady at the bank couldn't say enough nice things about you."

"I haven't slept with anyone since we got married, not even my wife. For the first time in my life I have a wife and I can't get her into bed." He raised one dark eyebrow and pointed out the one thing she wanted desperately to ignore. "You burn in my arms, Charlie."

"Me and half the women on this island." She practically ran off the boat.

CHARLOTTE INCREASED HER SPEED on the treadmill and tried to pretend it was a normal morning. Except Aaron was asleep in the next room. Last night had changed things. Changed her. Feelings buried deep inside had exploded. It was only a matter of time before her body betrayed her again.

Who had she been kidding thinking going to Aaron was a logical decision? It had been lust, pure and simple. She'd never be able to face him.

Aaron had followed her to the bungalow and slept beside her, but they had avoided conversation like a curse. She hadn't moved a muscle all night for fear of waking him and what he might do. Or worse, how she might respond.

But he hadn't been the one doing the seducing. That dubious honor had been hers. She stomped through her morning routine, trying to work out her frustration.

Who was that woman on the boat? Was he sleeping with her? He said he wasn't, but all men lied about their affairs, didn't they? Perry certainly had. Her father. Rumor was, even Edward had kept a mistress when he was younger.

She dabbed at the sweat on her temples. None of this should matter. This wasn't a real marriage. In a few months they'd be divorced and he'd be back to his old life and she'd be back to—to what?

Slowing her pace, Charlotte tried to picture her future. If she lost the resort, if she upset her grandfather, there was nothing. No career, no financial security—no identity.

There were other hotels, but all her life she'd worked toward owning this resort. Now that it was finally within her grasp, she'd do whatever it took to keep it. She would not let

Perry Thurman win. She was a Harrington and no matter what cunning tricks Perry orchestrated, he wasn't.

She resumed her speed on the treadmill. When the resort was hers, the first order of business would be to fire Perry. She'd ease back into a routine, with no one to hassle her. Not Edward and his desire for her to settle down with a family. Not Perry and his subtle attempts to discredit her and take control of the resort. And most of all, not Aaron Brody and his sexual games. Life would be simple again.

She stepped off and grabbed a towel. Gee, that sounded exciting. Schedule romantic getaways for other couples all day, and then come home to an empty house at night.

Wonderful, completely euphoric!

Aaron's footsteps, muffled by the plush carpet, stopped beside the treadmill.

"Don't."

"Don't what?" he asked, his husky voice sounding so sexy she wanted to scream.

"Don't make it worse by talking about it. Last night didn't happen," she insisted, praying he'd understand her humiliation and drop the subject. Her well-organized, controlled life had erupted into a monumental disaster.

She blotted the perspiration off her neck.

"It did, you know," Aaron whispered.

She closed her eyes. "What?"

"Happen."

CHARLOTTE AND PERRY HAD FINISHED a quick sandwich at her desk and were going over staff responsibilities when Aaron opened the door.

Charlotte turned to Perry. "Give us a minute."

He stood and met Aaron at the door, sizing him up as he would a dangerous animal. "Afternoon, Brody."

Narrowing his eyes, Aaron watched Perry leave. Strolling

into the office wearing a clean pair of shorts and a dusty-green T-shirt, Aaron glanced at the two empty plates. "Guess I'm too late to invite you to lunch."

Thank God. "Did you get the engine out?"

He shook his head. "Can't get an engine lift until four."

They might as well be talking about the weather, but Charlotte would discuss anything to avoid the awkward silence. "I saw they were refinishing the outside."

"Yeah, they're scraping barnacles and polishing the hull." He glanced toward the window. "I may be late tonight." This was not the typical smart-mouthed Aaron.

Aaron left Charlie's office and made his way out of the resort. He was beginning to suspect she regretted her rash decision to marry him instead of Thurman. Why should he care? Just concentrate on the boat, Brody. Charlie could take care of herself.

As he started around the outside cabana bar, he heard a familiar voice. "It's only temporary."

Thurman? Aaron stopped just in time to keep from being seen. He stepped back behind the thatch wall. Thurman continued to spout off into his cell phone.

"Charlotte will never stay married to this lowlife. She only did it to fool the old man."

Aaron peered around the cabana to see if Thurman looked as cocky as he sounded. "The doctor in Monte Carlo told Harrington that with his heart, if he didn't get out from under this stress he'd be dead within a year. I don't see him slowing down and I intend to be in place when he drops."

He turned and Aaron ducked back behind the cabana. So, Thurman was banking on Harrington's heart condition. "I don't have to do much. She and Brody are already fighting. This guy's used to bedding hookers and Charlotte doesn't know how to do anything but lie there and tolerate it," he sneered. "He's after her money."

Aaron clenched his fist to keep from yanking the phone out of Thurman's hand and shoving it down his throat. All in good time. Thurman would pay.

CHARLOTTE'S FEET ACHED and all she wanted was to go home and crash. It was past eleven and she reached for her purse to leave.

Perry sauntered into her office. "Doesn't Aaron worry when you're late?"

Over the past week since the boat escapade, Charlotte had barely seen Aaron. She pretended to be asleep when he came in, usually sometime after midnight, and he was still sleeping when she left the next morning. In a way, it worked.

"My marriage is not your concern."

He thumbed through the stack of mail in her tray. "I scheduled one more clerk on the morning shift. We have another large tour checking out early. I don't know how you managed to run this place before I got here. In Monte Carlo, I never had these problems."

Charlotte flinched. Every corner she turned, Perry was there, waiting for her to slip up. He lurked in the shadows like a spy. Oh, he put on a good show of being helpful. But the less she involved him, the less opportunity for him to sabotage her. Still, he didn't miss a single opportunity to mention that he hadn't seen Aaron around. Her excuses were beginning to wear thin. At least Edward had left.

Charlotte glimpsed a parchment envelope as Perry flipped through the mail. Her lawyer's stationery? She yanked the mail out of his hands. "Maybe that explains why you can't deal with them here."

Catching a slight movement from the corner of her eye, she found Aaron leaning against her door. In a pair of faded jeans and a white T-shirt, he was a flawless picture of classic masculinity. It was sinful for a man to look that good.

"Brody." Perry tore his gaze away from the mail in her hand, and then headed out the door.

"Thurman."

Aaron studied Charlotte. She looked exhausted. Worried. For the first time in a week, he saw a nick in the emotionless businesswoman and a glimpse of the vulnerable girl he'd almost made love to. Subconsciously she squeezed the back of her neck. The memory of her heated flesh haunted him. He could still feel her thighs bracketing his. Still see the desire smoldering in her eyes.

He'd given her space, waiting for her to come to him again, but she'd retreated behind her cool, workaholic demeanor.

Something was going on, something more than placating her eccentric grandfather. "You okay?"

Leaning her head against the back of her chair, she sighed. "It's been a rough day."

Wanting to touch her, curious how she'd respond, Aaron stepped behind her desk and began massaging her neck and shoulders. The tension had her muscles bunched so tight he was amazed she could turn her neck. "You look done in. Relax."

She rolled her head back and forth, groaning. "Mmm." Her stomach growled.

"You haven't eaten?"

Closing her eyes, she whispered, "A salad. Zelda brought me a salad for lunch."

He took her hand and pulled her to her feet. "Come on. I'll scramble you some eggs."

Shaking her head, she picked up her purse and locked her desk. "Not in my kitchen you won't. We'd be lucky to find coffee. Let's raid the restaurant leftovers."

Aaron waited while she locked up. "Guess there are some perks to this business."

She led the way into the kitchen. Her steps didn't have their usual assurance. While he waited for her to get the food, he lit the candle on the corner table.

She backed through the swinging doors with a tray of goodies. "Nice touch," she offered, heading toward the candle-light.

He helped her unload a bowl of boiled shrimp and a bottle of cocktail sauce from the tray. There were leftover artichoke hearts and lemon sauce, two rolls and a couple beers.

She went after plates and silverware.

"Better than scrambled eggs." Aaron popped a shrimp into his mouth.

She stood staring at the table, holding two napkin-wrapped sets of silverware and two plates.

"Sit down, Charlie." He grabbed the plates and held out her chair.

She dropped into her seat and reached for one of the beers. "You've been working hard, too."

Aaron grinned watching Charlie swig her beer straight out of the bottle. "No kidding. Got to get my boat back in the water. I'm booked solid for Spring Break."

"That's great, but you sound exhausted."

"Yeah, but it's done. The engine's in. The hull's refinished. Official launch party, Wednesday afternoon. You should come," he said with an enthusiasm that surprised him. Why did it suddenly seem so important that she see what he'd accomplished with her money?

"Good idea. We need to spend time together. I'm running out of excuses for Perry."

Great. The only reason she'd consider coming was to promote the pretense and win her precious resort. "Guess I haven't been focused on Thurman."

She scrubbed her hands across her eyes. "That's not what I meant."

He dipped a bite of artichoke in lemon sauce.

"Aaron, I'd love to be there, if I can get away. It's just that Perry has managed to stick his nose into every aspect of the hotel, trying to impress Edward."

"Just take off. Good food, drinks, company." He leaned back. "I'd like you to be there."

"Okay," she agreed, taking him by surprise.

One thing you could count on with Charlie. She was direct. "It's a date." Reaching across the table, he took her hand in his and whispered, "Don't turn around, but we've got an audience."

Chapter Eight

Except for the single candle and the filtered light from the kitchen, shadows blanketed the dining room. Was Perry actually watching?

Charlotte couldn't take her eyes off Aaron as he came around the table and tugged her up and into his arms. Not only his scorching lips, but everything about him sizzled.

He spread his legs and held her close, swaying to some imaginary tune. "Let's make Percy pant." Taking her hands, he guided them around his neck and then framed her face with his palms. His lips were gentle as they made a slow exploration of her eyelids, nose and cheeks, coming frustratingly close, but never quite tasting her lips. The clean masculine scent of soap intoxicated her.

One hand dropped to the small of her back. The other eased behind her neck, removed the clasp from her hair, and angled her face for a penetrating kiss.

"Don't panic, just play along." He slipped his hands beneath her bottom and hoisted her onto the table.

Sliding her skirt up to her waist, he pressed himself close. She gasped at the hard pressure of his denim-covered erection through her panties. If this was for effect, he was certainly getting into his role.

He unbuttoned her blouse and spread it open to his

hungry gaze. Instinctively, her body leaned in to cover her lack of cleavage.

"I'm taking off your blouse."

"Aaron, I don't think this is a good idea."

She shivered as he finished unbuttoning it and slid his hands inside. His fingers felt hot against her skin as the silk blouse rustled and tickled her skin. She heard a moan, and then realized the sound came from her.

He didn't seem to mind her lack of curves. His mouth trailed hot kisses over the exposed cleavage, but when he hooked his thumbs beneath her bra straps, she grabbed his wrists. "Slow down."

The room exploded into light. Her heart stopped. Once the spell was broken, she was mortified to find Perry staring at her. She clutched the front of her blouse together.

Aaron held her against his chest and turned a casual glance toward the door. "Evening, Percy."

"You two aren't worried about a customer catching you?" She felt the chill of his unnerving eyes. "Poor judgment, Charlotte."

"He's lonely," Aaron whispered loud enough for Perry to hear.

She trembled, but Aaron held her tight, cradling her face against his shoulder. "Hey, Percy, when you call Edward, let him know we're working on that great-grandson, will ya?"

"The name's Perry. Got that? Perry, not Percy."

Winking at Perry, Aaron nuzzled Charlotte's right ear. "Perry, would you mind catching the lights on your way out?"

Perry turned, hit the light switch, and slammed the door behind him.

Aaron tossed his head back and laughed. "I'd have left the lights on. No doubt he's headed for a cold shower."

"Oh, God." She hugged Aaron and giggled. She'd missed him. "Maybe he'll at least leave me alone on that front."

"You know, that's the first time I've heard you laugh. You should do it more." He returned her hug and offered a smile. "He's giving you grief about other things besides your poor taste in husbands?"

"Oh, he's putting on an Emmy-winning show of support, but he's trying to undermine every aspect of my job."

Placing her hands on his T-shirt-covered biceps, she eased off the table and buttoned her blouse. "We'd better get out of here before a guest wanders in."

She deposited the tray of dishes in the kitchen while Aaron wiped off the table and blew out the candle. She linked her fingers through his as they walked into the lobby, wondering if tonight might…

"Mrs. Brody, this gentleman needs to speak with a manager," the front desk clerk stuttered, nodding uncomfortably toward a uniformed officer standing at the end of the counter.

Charlotte snapped into work mode. "Yes, sir. Is there a problem?"

"I have a warrant for one of your guests. He got himself into a fight at the Boar's Head."

She closed her eyes, seeing her romantic evening going down the tube. Damn! "Aaron, you might as well go on home."

"Give me a call and I'll come walk you to the bungalow."

She noted the resignation on his face. There was more to him than sex appeal. The man had a sweet side, hidden beneath that macho exterior. Every moment she spent with him, she fell deeper under his spell. "Who knows how long this will take. I'll be fine."

THE NEXT DAY CHARLOTTE FOUND herself in the hotel from hell. The morning shift manager called in sick. Perry was nowhere in sight and Zelda wasn't at her desk, leaving Charlotte to deal with one catastrophe after the next. Zelda was never at her desk lately and the only time she could count on Perry being there was to see her screw up and offer a suggestion on how she should have handled things better.

Before she realized she'd missed lunch, it was already afternoon. Aaron poked his head in, grinning like a kid on Christmas morning. "Ready?"

The boat launching. God, she'd forgotten. Charlotte looked around desperately. She wanted to go. And she hated to disappoint Aaron. But there was nobody to leave in charge.

"I'm sorry." She shook her head. "Would you be too upset if I didn't make it?"

He raised one eyebrow. "Everyone expects to see my wife there. This little play works both ways."

"Your friends will be there. It's not that big of a deal if I don't show up."

His eyes narrowed and his tone sounded clipped. "Of course not. It's not your business."

Before she could respond, the chef barged through the door ranting in French. All she could decipher was the word *potato*. Aaron glared at them, turned on his heel, and left, almost running Zelda down in the doorway. Zelda looked pleased about something and Aaron's obvious temper caused her smug grin to widen.

"Where have you been for the last two hours?" Charlotte barked.

Zelda retreated, dropped into her chair, and shuffled a couple papers around her desk. "I took a long lunch. You weren't here, so I figured it'd be okay."

"You know what the hours are. Unless you get prior approval you will be in that seat, working. Got that?"

The girl picked up a nail file and scraped it across one of her long orange fingernails. "Got it, boss."

Staring at her secretary's tight, low-cut blouse, microskirt, and short spikes of hair that today had a weird purple tint,

Charlotte decided she needed a more forceful approach. "Tomorrow, I expect you on time and dressed appropriately. That means a skirt that covers your butt and no exposed cleavage. I don't intend to have this conversation again."

Continuing to grate the rough file across her nail, Zelda crossed her bare legs and blew dust off her nail. "Sure thing."

Charlotte bit her tongue. The snippy woman at the employment agency would laugh her off the island if she fired the girl and asked her to send someone else. Four assistants in three months was excessive even for Charlotte. She couldn't handle the added stress of training someone new right now. At least Zelda knew the software and was capable of structuring a proper sentence. Plus, she already knew how Charlotte liked her coffee.

She couldn't stand another minute. Grabbing her purse, Charlotte escorted the chef out and locked her door, meeting Perry in the outer office. She hated to leave him alone to accuse her of shirking her duties, but the look on Aaron's face stung. "See what you can do for Pierre," she instructed, nodding toward the chef. "Then contact the cleaning service and make sure the rooms are ready, even if you have to take off your coat and scrub toilets."

She handed Zelda a To Do list. "I'm going to the launching of my husband's boat. You will stay at your desk and answer the phone. Shouldn't be a problem since you've already taken your afternoon break."

The celebration had just gotten underway when Aaron looked up and saw Charlie come on deck. Judging by her scowl, she was looking for a fight. Most likely with him, but it was her choice to be married to her job. She tugged her rose-pink jacket away from her skin, raised her eyebrows, and gaped as two girls strolled past wearing thong bikinis.

Listening to Charlie's high heels clicking across the wood

deck in sharp contrast to everyone else's sneakers or flip-flops, he knew he'd made the right decision. Today was the day Charlie was going to loosen up. She'd be pissed, but life was too short to be so uptight.

He snagged a plastic cup of wine off the counter and made his way through the crowd to Charlie. "Give me your jacket."

"The boat looks fantastic." She slipped out of the jacket and handed it to him, taking the glass with her other hand.

"Brody's Charters is back on the water." He removed his new royal-blue cap and placed it on her head. He hated to cover up the beautiful blond highlights, but she needed to feel like part of the festivities. Taking her arm, he led her under the shade, grabbing another cap off the counter, and pulling it on. "Hungry? There might be some shrimp left."

She glanced at the buffet. "That fruit looks good."

He filled a plate with strawberries, cantaloupe, mango and blackberries. "Relax. Enjoy."

Raul handed Aaron a cold bottle of water and winked. "We're on?" He was the only one Aaron had let in on the plan.

"We're on." Watching Charlotte sweat, Aaron wished he could rush this shindig along. His friends never missed an opportunity to party, especially if someone else footed the bill. Still, it was eighty-five degrees and not a cloud in the sky. Not even a breeze to cool things down. Charlie fanned her face with the cap.

Someone changed the CD and Ricky Martin's "Livin' La Vida Loca" sizzled through the speakers. Rosa came down off the flybridge and danced Raul onto the center of the deck. The rest of the crowd didn't waste time joining them and Aaron wondered if he'd be able to get rid of everyone before tomorrow.

He nodded at Charlie. "Come on. Take your shoes off."

Kicking her shoes under the bench, she took his hand. "I've never been to a boat launching before. Do people always wear this few clothes?"

"Wait till they let their hair down." He twirled her onto the makeshift dance floor.

As they danced, she swiped her sticky forehead with the back of her hand. Little tendrils of sweat-drenched hair clung to her neck and forehead. Her white silk blouse was sleeveless, but Aaron could only imagine how sticky and uncomfortable those stockings must be.

He started to suggest she go below and change, but that would give away his plan.

By the end of the dance, Charlotte's French twist had wilted and her mascara smudged. He had to do something before she passed out. The sun beating down on the deck made it unbearable. Leading her to the only available seat under the canopy, he handed her another cold glass of wine.

He'd been planning this party for two weeks, but now it couldn't be over quick enough. These people had to get off his boat. As miserable as Charlie looked, she'd be heading for home and a shower any second. She might be accustomed to working her ass off, but she did it in air-conditioning.

Placing two fingers in his mouth, he whistled and nodded to Raul. "I appreciate all you guys turning out. It means a hell of a lot that you took your time to help launch the *Free Wind*." He picked up a stack of assorted white and royal-blue T-shirts and placed them on the counter. "Take a shirt. Hey, if it wears out, come back and get another one."

Charlie narrowed her eyes, but everyone else was already reaching for a shirt. "The first round of drinks at the Gecko's on me. It's too hot to stay on this tub in port."

"Let's take her out and see how she runs," Rosa suggested.

Shaking his head, Aaron pulled her close enough to whisper in her ear. "I intend to, but it's a private party."

Catching on, she glanced at Charlie, kissed Aaron's cheek, and winked. "See you tomorrow."

He shook a few hands and watched his friends shuffle across the gangplank. But when Charlie stood to leave, he grabbed her hand. "I know it's hot, but hang on. Let me give you a tour."

She smiled. "You've never told me much about the boat."

"What do you want to know? She's about thirty years old. Forty-four feet. Rock solid. Teak wood trim. New turbo-diesel."

Leading her to the controls, he started the engine. "Listen to that. Isn't that the most beautiful sound you've ever heard?"

Raul escorted the last guests off the boat, pitched the lines, and waved. Aaron eased the throttle forward, praying Charlie hadn't noticed. If he could pull far enough away from the dock, there wouldn't be anything she could do. "You haven't commented. What do you think?"

Grabbing the dash, her eyes widened. "It's moving."

He concentrated on maneuvering away from the dock and out of the marina. "Yeah, it is."

"But I have to work." Her knuckles turned white. "Aaron, take me back."

"Make Perry earn his keep. How much can the conniving jerk screw up in a few hours?"

She frowned and took her phone out of her purse.

He steered the boat to the right to avoid a sailboat of lobster-red tourists. "Put it away or I'll toss it overboard."

She ignored his threat and punched in a number. Before she could press the call button, Aaron swiped the phone out of her hand. "Relax, Charlie. I've got to pay attention here. Why don't you go below and put on something cooler?"

"I don't have anything cooler. I didn't realize I was going on a cruise." She grabbed her phone and shoved it into her purse.

"Look down in the cuddy."

"The what?" she snapped and clenched her jaw.

The corner of his mouth turned up. "Cabin, sweetheart. Go below and change. You look a little steamed."

She narrowed her eyes at the retreating shoreline. "I'm not amused. Take me back, Aaron."

"Ain't gonna happen, Charlie."

Charlotte went down the stairs, thinking of every disgusting name she could call him.

Kidnapping. That's what this was. She didn't think it was possible to be any angrier until she saw her clothes. Her black swimsuit, yellow shorts and striped T-shirt, that stupid sundress with the buttons, and a couple pairs of underwear spread across his bed in an artful array of color. He'd raided her underwear drawer! Was nothing sacred to this man?

The floor vibrated beneath her feet. Open water! She stood paralyzed, trying not to think about the rolling waves and unknown creatures lurking below. She fought for composure. She would not humiliate herself and let Aaron see her terror.

Chapter Nine

Charlotte peeled off her sticky clothes and dropped them in a heap on the floor. Sweat saturated her bra and panties. The suit was ruined. She tugged on clean underwear and the shorts, then pulled the knit shirt over her head. Aaron hadn't bothered to bring her a dry bra. Probably figured with her flat chest, why bother?

What was he up to with this little escapade? She hated surprises. Even as a child, she'd liked things planned out.

Climbing back on deck, she grasped the rail and tried to squelch her nausea as the boat lurched over a wave. She had to convince Aaron to take her home. The salty wind whipped at her hair and she struggled to hold the tangled tendrils out of her face. The boat skimmed across the water and the shoreline faded into the aqua water. "I'm not amused by this."

"You're the first person I've ever met who habitually resisted fun." He looked her up and down, his eyes smoldering. "At least you look more comfortable."

She narrowed her eyes. "Where are you taking me?"

"Private beach."

She grabbed the rail and avoided looking down at the spray. "There's a beach at the resort."

"Not like this one. We're going to have fun."

"I didn't tell anyone I was taking the rest of the day off. At the very least I should let Perry know I won't be back for a while."

He shrugged. "He's an educated man. He'll figure it out."

She sat down on one of the cushioned benches and gripped the shiny brass rail so tight her knuckles hurt. If she didn't think about the deep water beneath, maybe she'd get through this without making a fool of herself. She checked her watch. "How far are we going?"

"Relax. Chill."

Chill? She blew off steam and tried not to explode. Instead she closed her eyes and concentrated on slow, easy breaths. Obviously Aaron wasn't going to give in and take her back.

It seemed like an eternity before he cut the engine and dropped anchor. A white sandy beach shaded by tall palms outlined the tranquil cove. Leaning down, Aaron gave her a quick kiss and started putting the leftover party food away.

Charlotte released her grip on the rail and sucked air into her lungs. She tried to ignore the boat rocking, stood, and snapped the plastic lid on the bowl of fruit. "So how long did it take to mastermind this?"

He closed one mischievous green eye and pretended to think. "I decided last night when we almost made love in the restaurant."

"Is that what's on the agenda?" Her heart thudded.

"Maybe. If the mood strikes me."

"If the mood strikes you? I don't have a say in this?"

He grinned. "If it strikes me, I'll make sure it strikes you."

"You're fooling, right? You couldn't possibly be this arrogant."

Chuckling, he closed the refrigerator, yanked his T-shirt over his head, and unzipped his shorts.

She was relieved to see he wore a navy-blue boxer swimsuit. "Look, I'm sweltering, tired, and in no mood to sit out here and bake, no matter how beautiful the scenery." She blinked her eyes and diverted her gaze from his tanned chest.

Grabbing a bottle of water off the table, he took a swig and put it in the fridge. "Planning to swim in your shorts?"

"I'm not swimming."

He leaned forward and began a slow seduction of her mouth. No pressure or force, just simple, smoldering, mouth-to-mouth massage therapy. Stepping back, he selected a perfect purple orchid out of a wilting flower arrangement from the party. "There's nobody watching this time. Let's just relax and enjoy the day. What do you say?"

Accepting the flower, she allowed the seductive pull of his deep voice to melt the last of her irritation. How could she want to throttle him one second and melt at his touch the next?

Tension dissolved as he removed her confining hair clip and his fingertips probed and massaged her scalp and neck.

She still held the orchid as he backed away and tugged the bottom of her shirt up and over her head. He took the flower long enough to pull her hand out of the sleeve, then brushed the flower lightly over her breasts, causing her nipples to harden. She shivered at being exposed in broad daylight.

Kicking a mat out from under one of the benches, he rolled it out on the wood deck. "Lie down."

That simmering desire in his eyes made her feel so sexy. So feminine. She no longer wanted to go back. As long as the boat wasn't moving, she wasn't afraid. Of all the places she could be right now, the *Free Wind* in this deserted cove ranked at the top of the list. Pretend or not, somehow she, Charlotte Harrington, had married the sexiest man in South Florida.

Stretching out on her stomach, she gave herself up to his magic hands. His palms pressed and prodded her tight muscles as he rubbed circles of cool coconut lotion into her skin. Arms—neck—shoulders—back. She listened to the gulls squawking overhead as he slipped her shorts off.

If his scuba business sunk, he had another marketable skill. The bottom of her feet—calves—knees—thighs. She heard his swimsuit drop to the deck. She was in tune to the squeak of the lotion bottle as he squirted more into his hands before she felt the silken touch on her buttocks. The warm moisture between her legs had nothing to do with the lotion or the humid heat and everything to do with Aaron Brody's strong legs straddling hers, intimately pressing against her thighs.

As his hands worked their way beneath her to stimulate and fondle, she raised her hips, craving his touch. His aroused body touched her hip and she bit her lip to keep from begging. She wanted him inside her, but he teased and took his sweet time. He rolled her over and continued to play the part of seductive masseur. Breasts—tummy—

Closing her eyes, she welcomed the brunt of his weight. "Mmm," she sighed, as he slid inside her. There was one part of his anatomy that wielded even more magic than his hands. Her hips moved in unison with his. She reveled in the sensation of having his body both inside and wrapped around her. Hot, licking flames ignited every inch of her. She groaned when he pulled away for protection, but was eager to welcome him back. She didn't remember sex being like this.

There was power in each thrust of his hips. He consumed her with the sheer ecstasy of making love for the pure, erotic enjoyment of the act. No games, no thought, just sweaty skin against sweaty skin. She could taste salt in his kiss as their bodies melded together in the quest for bliss.

She exploded. Her heart pounded and the only breath she could draw came directly from his mouth. She wrapped her legs around his hips, arched her back, and invited him deeper. All she could see, feel or think was Aaron.

He squeezed his eyes shut and buried his face in her neck. He stilled and then relaxed against her.

Even in the shade of the boat canopy, the tropical heat took her breath. But, she wasn't willing to turn him loose. His tanned skin shimmered with perspiration and his damp hair curled in the humidity.

Cupping his hips, she held him tight. "Don't leave."

He was already pulling back. "I don't have the strength left to hold myself up." He eased over on his side, taking her with him. Cradling her into the crook of his arm, he planted a kiss on top of her head. "Oh, man."

Perspiration trickled down her back and she was sticky from head to toe, but it didn't matter. With one finger, she traced a wet curl plastered to his forehead. The tendril corkscrewed around the tip of her finger in a tight caress. Dark, sooty lashes accented his intense green eyes.

Rolling over on his back, he took her with him and pushed her up until she was straddling him. He reached to the side and handed her the bottle of suntan lotion. "Your turn."

She grinned, squirting a dollop of lotion into her hand. "You don't need this. All mine is on you already."

As she lathered the lotion between her hands, her phone chimed. Before she could reach it, Aaron grabbed the phone out of her purse and pushed the button. "You have reached the cell phone of Charlie Brody," his deep voice advised whoever was on the other end. "She is otherwise occupied and unable to come to the phone at the moment, but if you'd hang up she'd be very appreciative." He disconnected.

She swiped the lotion off her hand onto his chest and retrieved her phone. Pressing the button to view the last caller, her mouth fell open. "You hung up on Edward."

"I'm sure he'll be delighted," Aaron assured her with a wry grin, taking the phone and turning the power off.

He stood up wearing nothing but his God given glory, scooped her into his arms, and started toward the rail.

"No! Don't," she shrieked as he tossed her over the side.

Her heart stopped and she clawed at air, plunging toward the water. Before she could orient herself to figure out which way was up, Aaron landed in a tornado of bubbles beside her. She plowed her way to the surface and grabbed for him, struggling to grasp his oily shoulders.

"Whoa, slow down. It's okay." He wrapped one arm securely around her waist.

She clutched frantically. "Don't let go."

"There's nothing to be afraid of. It's not that deep and you can see the bottom."

His arm stayed around her waist until she eased her choke hold on his neck and looked down. The water was the color of an aquamarine gemstone, crystal clear and shimmering. There weren't any waves in the cove. She counted to twenty until her breathing regulated. Self-consciously, she moved out of his hold and began treading water on her own.

His eyes watched her, waiting for her to freak out again. "Sorry about that. The boat's right here," he said.

"I'm fine. I just prefer pools."

"This isn't much different than a big swimming pool and I'm here. Come on, one lap around the boat."

She swam beside him, beginning to enjoy the feel of the cool water against her heated skin. So much more freedom than a pool. And there was something magical about swimming in the nude. If she could only keep her mind off crushing waves and inky water.

Aaron retrieved snorkels and masks from the diving platform and proceeded to teach her to breathe as she swam. Charlotte had snorkeled once or twice, but it had been years.

None of the flashy brochures at the resort did justice to the beauty of the underwater world of the coral reef. Charlotte pointed to a bunch of long skinny coral. "What's that?"

"Sea finger coral," Aaron replied. "Next to that is a clump of brain coral."

She stuck her face back in the water, before lifting it to comment. "Did you see those pink fish?"

"Creole Wrasse. Sometimes you can see angel fish, too."

The bright fish flitted in and out through a vibrant, living playground of coral. "You're a regular coral reef encyclopedia."

Once she got over the initial shock, the warm, tropical water seemed as comfortable as a huge bathtub. She even saw a giant manatee. And Aaron was never far from her side.

The afternoon was the nearest thing to freedom Charlotte could remember. Never in her wildest dreams had she imagined frolicking nude in the Atlantic Ocean. That was a stunt her parents would've pulled.

Her inhibitions faded as they floated and played like kids in their private cove. When she wrapped her legs around her Adonis's waist and lowered herself onto him, the surprised grin on his face was worth her effort.

Reacting to her impulses, she made love to Aaron with sunshine beating down on her already heated skin and nothing between them but gorgeous azure water.

AARON TIMED DINNER TO COINCIDE with the sunset. He wanted Charlie to remember the afternoon long after he was out of her life. For some reason, how she remembered him had become very important.

They sat on the dive deck at the back of the boat, dangling their feet in the water and nibbling on the party leftovers. Her thick ponytail poked out the back of a royal-blue Brody's Charters cap. She looked happy, healthy and relaxed for the first time in the three years he'd known her.

The new deck provided the perfect observation point. There were enough clouds to give the sunset character, brush-strokes of pink and purple transforming the sky into a contemporary mural. Probably rain by morning.

Shaking his head, he allowed the salty breeze to blow his

hair back, dipped a strawberry in his plastic glass of wine, and popped the fruit into her mouth. "Nothing compares to sunsets in the Keys."

"Nothing?" She bit into the strawberry and pink juice squirted down her chin.

He watched mesmerized as she wiped it away with the back of her hand. "Well, almost nothing." He got hard just thinking about the feel of her beneath him, the taste of salt on her skin, that little moan.

"Look." She pointed toward the horizon and grinned. "Dolphins. Two of them."

"Yeah, sometimes they'll come right up to the boat."

He took a deep, cleansing breath of sea air as the giant orange ball kissed the horizon and melted into the water. He ran his hands through his hair and watched the gulls light for the night. God, it was heaven out here with Charlie.

When he suggested they spend the night on the boat, she didn't put up a fight. He agreed to wake up at sunrise to take her back, but they had tonight. The cabin was stuffy, but she didn't seem to mind the sticky heat as she snuggled against his chest and drifted off to sleep.

Maybe they wouldn't go back. Let Edward keep his resort. Yeah, like Charlie would ever choose him over running Harrington's.

He tightened his arms around his wife as she tucked her head into the crook of his shoulder. What are you thinking, Brody? It's not like he wanted anything permanent. Did he?

A BOOMING CLAP OF THUNDER shook the cabin and jolted Charlotte from her peaceful dream. She stared at the skylight above the small berth and clutched the mattress. A bright flash of lightning streaked through the sky. It was storming and she was in the middle of the ocean!

The boat rocked and another clap of thunder reverberated

through the cabin. The rain pelted against the skylight and the berth tilted as the front rose, and then slammed back level. Grabbing Aaron's arm, she shook him. "Wake up. It's storming."

"Sounds that way," he yawned.

How could he be so calm? The air cracked with electrical current and the cabin exploded with light, then returned to gray.

They had to get off this boat—now! But how? There was no protection on shore. Heading across the turbulent ocean in the middle of a storm terrified her nearly as much as riding it out. She shivered. The damp confines of the tiny cabin closed in around her.

She bolted out of bed. The boat lurched and she lost her balance.

Aaron reached out and tried to urge her back down on the bed. "Let's try this again and wake up slow this time. There's no rush. It's hardly past five. What's another half hour?"

"I can't stay here!" She grabbed the bathroom door and held on. The waves were bigger than yesterday. She could feel the boat bobbing.

"What's wrong, sweetheart?" He sat up and rubbed his eyes.

"Where're the life jackets? How're we going to get back?"

Crawling out of bed, he slipped his arms around her. "We have plenty of life jackets and we'll go back the same way we got here. But the sun's barely up. We've got time." He nibbled at her shoulder. "You're trembling."

"I hate storms. I hate storms on the ocean."

He handed her a pair of panties. "It's a thunderstorm. No big deal." He slipped a white Brody's Charters T-shirt over her head.

She sat on the berth and tugged on her underwear. "Look, Aaron, find me a life jacket and get us back to the mainland. Okay? Can you do that?" She hated the crack in her voice.

Retrieving a life jacket from beneath the bench that served as one side of the kitchen booth, he squatted down in front of her, and buckled her into it. "There's nothing to be afraid of. We're safe."

She clenched her fists to still her hands. "When I was six, my parents took me sailing. A storm blew up and waves were crashing over the deck and sucking at my legs. I kept clinging to this pole, but I couldn't hold on. The pole was wet and slipped out of my hands. I grabbed for anything to hold on to, but I went over. The salt water burned my eyes and I couldn't see the boat. I just kept screaming and screaming, but I didn't think anyone heard me. My dad jumped in and his buddy pulled us out."

He reached out and rested his hand along one side of her face. "It's okay. You're not going overboard today."

She leaned into his hand, but her throat closed up and she couldn't say any more.

There was no trace of fear as he continued. "This storm isn't that bad. It'll pass."

She clutched the mattress. "You don't get it. I've spent thousands of dollars in therapy and I can't kick this. Get me off this water."

Taking her by the shoulders, he stared deep into her eyes. "I've been on the water practically every day since I was fifteen and I've weathered lots of storms worse than this, on this very boat." He tucked her hair behind her ear. "Would you rather lie down and let me hold you until this passes? The water's calmer in the cove."

"I want to go back," she begged. "Can we do that?"

"Sure. Just relax." He stood up and slipped on his shorts and T-shirt. "I've done this a thousand times."

Nodding, she curled up on the berth and tried to keep from shaking. Relaxing was out of the question. She'd settle for not throwing up.

Chapter Ten

Aaron climbed on deck, lifted anchor, and started the engine. Would Charlie be okay? Lots of people were afraid of storms, but she was on the verge of hysterics. He felt like the world's biggest brute for tossing her overboard yesterday. But he'd had no idea. He tuned in the radio for a weather report. Sounded like the storms were here for the day. The rational answer would be to ride it out in the cove, but Charlie would have a heart attack if she had to spend an entire day in the state she was in.

The waves were going to be rough once they hit open water. Nothing he couldn't navigate, but more than enough to toss the boat around. It had been a great escape until this.

Keeping one eye on the gauges and the other on the waves, he tried to listen for Charlie in case she needed him. Pulling out of the cove wasn't bad until they rounded the point and caught the full brunt of the wind. Still, if it weren't for her, he wouldn't be concerned. It'd be slow going, but they'd get there.

They were halfway to shore when she came and stood beside him. She grabbed the console and slipped her other arm around his waist. She focused straight-ahead. "This is bad, isn't it?"

"Just tropical wind and rain. We're under control." He offered her a reassuring smile, hooked a deck chair with his foot, and motioned her to sit. Up here she was protected from the sea spray and if she stayed seated, maybe she wouldn't see the waves. "Sure you don't want to stay below?"

"No, I'd rather be close to you." She reached down and took the life jacket off the hook. "You need to put this on."

He started to decline, but after one look at her pale, drawn face, he slipped his arms through the straps. He reached over and massaged the back of her neck, keeping his voice calm. "Talk to me. Keep me company."

She stretched her neck to check the waves, then focused on him. Her knuckles were white from the death grip she had on the arms of the chair. "My parents were thrill seekers. They wanted us kids to experience everything. I did fine with snow skiing and snowmobiles. Even parachuted out of an airplane." She grinned. "We saw every kind of race, cars, horses, dogs, anything they could bet on. I was fine until they insisted we go white-water rafting. They didn't understand my fear."

"Sounds like you had a hell of a childhood. I never got out of South Florida." He focused on the choppy waves.

"Yeah, but the only stability we had were my grandparents. My parents didn't want kids. I'm sure Edward pressured them, like he's pressuring me. Since they already had a son to carry on the Harrington lineage, you've got to know I was an accident."

"I doubt you were unwanted."

"They didn't have time for Don and me. They were too busy partying."

The boat pitched, but he ignored the jolt and pretended they were on smooth water. "So how serious is Edward's heart condition?"

Charlotte cocked her head. "He doesn't have a heart condition."

"I heard Perry talking on his cell telling someone that

The Harlequin Reader Service — Here's how it works:

Accepting your 2 free books and 2 free gifts (gifts valued at approximately $10.00) places you under no obligation to buy anything. You may keep the books and gifts and return the shipping statement marked "cancel". If you do not cancel, about a month later we'll send you 4 additional books and bill you just $4.24 each in the U.S. or $4.99 each in Canada. That is a savings of 15% off the cover price. It's quite a bargain! Shipping and handling is just 25¢ per book. You may cancel at any time, but if you choose to continue, every month we'll send you 4 more books, which you may either purchase at the discount price or return to us and cancel your subscription.

*Terms and prices subject to change without notice. Prices do not include applicable taxes. Sales tax applicable in N.Y. Canadian residents will be charged applicable provincial taxes and GST. Offer not valid in Quebec. Credit or debit balances in a customer's account(s) may be offset by any other outstanding balance owed by or to the customer. Please allow 4 to 6 weeks for delivery. Offer available while quantities last.

If offer card is missing write to: Harlequin Reader Service, P.O. Box 1867, Buffalo NY 14240-1867
or visit www.ReaderService.com

NO POSTAGE
NECESSARY
IF MAILED
IN THE
UNITED STATES

BUSINESS REPLY MAIL
FIRST-CLASS MAIL   PERMIT NO. 717   BUFFALO, NY

POSTAGE WILL BE PAID BY ADDRESSEE

HARLEQUIN READER SERVICE
PO BOX 1867
BUFFALO NY 14240-9952

GET FREE BOOKS and FREE GIFTS
WHEN YOU PLAY THE...

Just scratch off the silver box with a coin. Then check below to see the gifts you get!

SLOT MACHINE GAME!

YES! I have scratched off the silver box. Please send me the 2 free Harlequin American Romance® books and 2 free gifts (gifts are worth about $10) for which I qualify. I understand I am under no obligation to purchase any books, as explained on the back of this card.

354 HDL EXAH   154 HDL EXC5

FIRST NAME	LAST NAME

ADDRESS

APT.#	CITY

STATE/PROV.	ZIP/POSTAL CODE

7 7 7 — Worth **TWO FREE BOOKS** plus 2 **BONUS** Mystery Gifts!

🍒🍒🍒 — Worth **TWO FREE BOOKS!**

♣♣♣ — Worth **ONE FREE BOOK!**

🔔🔔🍒 — **TRY AGAIN!**

www.ReaderService.com

(H-AR-07/09)

with Edward's heart and the stress he was under, he wouldn't last long." Aaron held tight as they rolled over a large swell. "I also saw him taking medication at the wedding, but I figured you knew."

She closed her mouth. "I'm his own granddaughter and I had no idea. Why wouldn't he tell me something like that?"

The concern on her face was admirable given the way Edward treated her. "Thurman also said he'd be married to you and running Harrington's within a year."

Her brow furrowed. "Now Perry's resurgence of interest in marrying me fits. But how did he find out about Edward?"

"Beats me. Think that's why Edward's so hung up on you having a baby, male no less?"

"Out of four children, Edward was the only son. He and Grandmother were only able to conceive one child, my dad, and he's dead. Who's going to carry on the Harrington legacy?"

"If carrying on the Harrington legacy is so important, I'd think he'd pressure your brother."

"After Don moved in with his latest companion, Gerald, Edward finally gave up." Her eyes focused on his steering. "You've been working on a boat since you were fifteen?"

He shrugged. "Whistler, the old man who owned the *Free Wind,* put me to work. I hauled scuba tanks, sold drinks, held customers' heads while they barfed. Basic gofer stuff."

Her cute little nose turned up. "What about school?"

"What about it?" Aaron avoided the subject of education and still tried to keep her mind off the storm. She was beginning to relax, at least the color had returned to her knuckles. "Whistler died of emphysema three years ago. Left the boat to me. Seemed like a good time for a change of scenery."

She offered a shaky smile. "So Whistler was a father figure after your mom died?"

"Uh, not exactly." He scratched his neck and smiled at the

memory. "That old man could cuss with the sailors, drink any man under the table, and fight anyone left standing. Always had a cigarette hanging out of his mouth."

"Doesn't sound like much of a role model for a young boy."

"Young boy?" He wondered if he'd ever fit that description. "I needed a job and a roof over my head."

"Did he teach you to dive?"

"About the time I hired on, he was beginning to have trouble breathing. Hell, he had trouble waking up before noon, if he made it home at all. Later it was the emphysema that kept him above water."

"Aaron, you're a caretaker." She sounded pleased with her summation.

"You make me sound like someone's grandmother."

"First you took care of your mom, then Whistler."

The bow bucked and tossed, popped over the crest of a large swell, and slammed hard on the other side. Aaron was careful not to show any sign of nervousness as he maneuvered the boat back on course. Charlie's face went chalk-white. Just five more minutes and they'd be to shore.

Keep talking, Brody. Keep her mind off the storm. "Everyone knew where to find me when Whistler needed help. I bailed him out of jail, hauled him home drunk two out of three nights. Once I talked a seven-foot sailor out of mopping up the floor with him when Whistler made some wisecrack about the guy's mother." He laughed. "Whistler was five-foot-eight, tops. A hundred pounds, soaking wet. He was a character."

"See, you are a caretaker."

"Maybe. That's probably why he shelled out the money for me to get my certification. Well, that and his health had gotten so bad he couldn't dive anymore. I ended up in the water while he handled the money. No complaints from me there."

"Did you ever dream of doing anything else?"

Aaron swallowed. She was getting too damn curious!

He pulled the *Free Wind* into his slip and killed the engine. Someone with Charlie's education would never understand that even the simplest dreams were so far out of his grasp it wasn't worth trying. Thanks to his dyslexia, simply getting through the written test to become a certified diver had been grueling. The last thing he wanted was Charlie's pity. "I don't know. Maybe."

The sky was ominous with rain peppering down and painting the deserted dock ten shades darker. Not many people ventured out on rainy days. The tourists shopped or took advantage of indoor resort activities while the men who normally kept the dock buzzing took a deserved day off.

He secured the boat and then looked at Charlie. Her color had returned. "You okay?"

She stood by the wheel watching him with the strangest expression. He couldn't read her. Walking toward him, she wrapped both arms around his waist and pressed her body against his wet T-shirt. "I didn't realize what you were doing. I forgot to be scared."

He leaned down and gave her a gentle kiss. God, how long had it been since anyone had looked at him with such trust?

EDWARD HAD A HEART PROBLEM. Charlotte dropped the towel and pulled her slip over her head, but she couldn't concentrate on dressing for work. Men like her grandfather didn't get sick. Edward was her rock. It had never crossed her mind that he wouldn't always be there.

She sat on the edge of the bed and buried her face in her hands. "How could he not tell me something like this? Does he have to keep everything inside?"

"Pride." Aaron squatted down in front of her offering a steaming cup of coffee.

So absorbed in her worries, she hadn't realized she'd spoken aloud. "Too proud to share his fears with his closest relative?"

He set the coffee on the nightstand and took her hand. "Too proud to admit weakness."

Charlotte winced. She could relate to that, but it seemed so sad from this side of the relationship. "He obviously told Perry."

"I doubt it. Not sure how Thurman found out, but I'd take bets Edward didn't tell him."

That realization offered some comfort. She sniffed. "This changes everything. It all makes sense now." Her rock was crumbling.

"What? Edward wanting you at head office learning the business?"

"And married to Perry. He doesn't think women have the makeup to run his empire." She'd just have to prove him wrong. How could she not move back to Boston now? Someone had to step up and learn the ropes. And that person was not going to be Perry Thurman.

"Charlie, are you okay?"

She swiped at the tears running down her cheeks. "It's over. Whatever hope I had for independence is history." She shoved her wet hair back. "I have to protect Harrington's. My brother sure isn't going to do it. I think Don would get some perverted thrill watching Edward's empire crumble."

There'd never been a doubt in Charlotte's mind that eventually she would step up and run the family business. She'd been preparing to run Harrington's her entire life.

But for just a moment, being with Aaron, she'd seen a glimpse of freedom from the daunting responsibility she'd been groomed for.

Aaron wound a strong, comforting arm around her waist, making her wish with every feminine instinct she had that this pretend marriage was real.

"Okay, so tell your granddad whatever it is you know about Thurman. Give him facts."

She stared up at the ceiling. "If it were only that simple. He'd discount anything I said at this point. The only way he'll get rid of Perry is if I present an undisputable case or he sees with his own eyes how unscrupulous the man is."

"That shouldn't be too hard to arrange," Aaron said with a cocky grin.

Chapter Eleven

Charlotte rubbed the back of her neck and flipped to the next report. Reviewing the monthly financials had never seemed so arduous. Or so important. There was no way in hell she'd allow Perry to take over Harrington's. Harrington's was her legacy, her identity. It was who she was.

Until Aaron.

Over the past week she'd become a different woman, sultry and sexy. Nights blazed with passion in Aaron's arms. But during the day, she still fought for her place in the family business.

"If the grocer can't fill your orders correctly, change suppliers," Perry said.

She ground her back teeth. "What do you suggest? I have them FedExed from Miami?"

"Water usage is up," he stated, moving on to the next item.

"So are occupancy and income," Charlotte countered.

The sunlight filtering into her office window faded steadily. She frowned at the clock. Seven-thirty already? She pictured Aaron waiting at the bungalow and longed for the sanctuary of home.

Perry scrawled red ink on another page of his yellow tablet. The reports already resembled the scene of a brutal massacre. If Edward put him in charge, every Harrington resort manager would race for the door within a month.

"Perry, we'll continue this tomorrow. I'm beat. With the exception of groceries, everything is in line."

"Really?" Leaning back in his chair, Perry tapped the red pen on the edge of the desk. Tappity-tap. "Then maybe you'd like to explain this." He tossed a copy of the loan document on the desk.

Her heart plummeted. Before she could respond the office door opened and Aaron walked in. "It's late. You two still working?"

She took a deep breath and unclenched her fists. "Just finishing up."

Aaron frowned as he walked toward her. "Charlie?"

Perry gathered the reports and loan document and tapped them on the desk, then placed them neatly in his briefcase. "Nice to see you, Brody. By the way, the boat looks great." As Perry passed, he caressed Charlotte's shoulder. She flinched. "We'll continue this tomorrow. Have a nice evening."

Aaron waited until the door closed behind Perry. "What the hell was that all about?"

If Edward got wind of the loan, he'd realize this marriage was a farce and ruin Aaron. She didn't know how, but Edward was ruthless. When someone spit in his face, he took great enjoyment in finding their weakness and destroying them.

She couldn't stop trembling. Did Perry know about the prenuptial, too? She had to stop him from telling her grandfather.

"Perry's playing mind games, as usual."

He kneaded her shoulders. "Do you always tremble like that when he upsets you?"

Shaking her head, she reached for her purse. "Can this wait? I've got a pounding headache." The last thing she needed was to get into this here and have Perry overhear.

WHEN THEY ARRIVED AT the bungalow, Aaron seated her at the kitchen table and opened the fridge. He took out a bowl of fresh strawberries, followed by an identical bowl of pineapple chunks. He retrieved a plate and set it in front of her, then a fork and a glass of white wine. Speechless, she watched him slice cheese and pull a box of crackers from the cabinet.

She popped a bite of pineapple into her mouth and tried not to sigh. "You had groceries delivered?"

He flashed her an odd look. "I walked down to the store. Figured it'd be nice to have food in the house."

He'd gone grocery shopping. Men really did that? When was the last time she'd shopped? Charlotte bit into a plump strawberry, then grabbed a napkin and swiped at the juice running down her hand.

Twisting the top off a beer, he watched her eat. "Obviously Thurman was his typical asshole self tonight."

"He knows about the loan. Maybe not what it's for, but it's only a matter of time. We have to find something concrete on him soon or it's going to be too late. Edward's considering making him CFO."

Aaron took a swig of beer. "It's got to be more than a few mishandled reservations for the old man to fire him."

She swallowed one more bite of pineapple and snapped the lid back on the bowl. "You're right, but what?" There had to be a way to stop Perry before she found herself working for him.

"Want me to take Thurman for a one-way cruise? I could pick one of the Keys that sinks at high tide and drop him off with a bottle of suntan lotion and a picnic basket, then forget to go back."

Watching him sip his beer, she smiled. A couple curls had fallen across his forehead and his eyes were so gorgeous. He was a good guy. He didn't deserve to lose his business. If she lost her resort, she'd survive somehow. There was always another hotel, but the charter boat was all Aaron had. How would he earn a living if Edward destroyed his business?

There wasn't any choice. She had to tell Edward about the money before Perry did.

WHEN EDWARD ANSWERED HIS CELL, she heard restaurant commotion. "Good morning, Grandfather. Just wanted to let you know I'm e-mailing you some pictures of the *Free Wind.*" She held her breath.

"Aaron's boat?"

"It looks wonderful. New engine. New paint. You won't recognize it. His business is already picking up."

"So now you're taking out loans and funding Brody's business."

She'd known Perry wouldn't waste any time. "He's my husband and we want his charters to be an asset to Harrington's. The boat has to meet our standards, you know."

"We need to talk about that. From what Perry said on our morning call, Harrington standards aren't being met in a lot of ways at Marathon."

What morning call? The rat was further in than she'd even thought. "I've been running Marathon without fault for almost five years. Why do you think I need Perry looking over my shoulder?"

"I don't trust Brody. And from the way Perry described the books, it's a good thing he's there."

With Perry around, it was *Aaron* Edward chose not to trust? "You've never had issues with my numbers before. Now that Perry's here, you do? Don't you think it's overkill to waste the skill of two managers down here? I know you're short since Harvey Lattimer retired," Charlotte pointed out.

Edward hesitated. "Are you asking to be transferred? Is everything all right with Aaron?"

"I wasn't talking about me. Seems like Perry's needed more in Chicago where you don't have a manager."

"Perry is staying in Marathon. I have my reasons."

"Because you don't trust Aaron? Or is it me you don't trust?"

"Are you questioning my judgment?" His tone became clipped.

"You're questioning mine."

"If you have an issue working with Perry, then I can easily find somewhere else to utilize your skills."

"I manage this resort."

Edward snapped. "Well, then you should have enough foresight to realize Perry is helping straighten out some serious problems. I've had two formal complaints in the last month."

"The month that Perry's been in place, I might add."

"Perry ran the Monte Carlo resort without a single complaint the entire six years he was there. You could learn a lot from his experience, his professionalism."

Charlotte cringed.

"I'm late for a meeting. Is there anything else?" he challenged in a chilling, professional tone.

"No." Charlotte dropped the phone in the cradle and stared at it in disbelief. If Edward had one more reason to question her ability, Perry would end up running Harrington's, not just Marathon.

She dialed the Monte Carlo resort, but the manager was on holiday. She had to find out why Perry had really left.

AARON DOCKED THE *FREE WIND* and handed out T-shirts to the eight college kids who'd booked today's charter. It had been an exceptional dive. One of the guys had actually proposed to his girlfriend in the cove and the entire afternoon had become one big celebration.

He turned on the hose and squinted into the bright blue sky

as he sprayed down the deck. The newly engaged couple's love couldn't have been clearer if it'd blazed in neon. That was what Edward Harrington was looking for between him and Charlotte. Aaron grinned. The old man had left town too soon.

Love. Since he'd first made love to Charlie, Aaron had almost forgotten that this marriage was all a farce. But he needed to keep reminding himself that in a few months, she'd no longer be his wife.

"Hi."

Aaron spun, almost spraying Charlie instead of the deck. "Sorry," he said, turning off the hose and dropping it on the deck.

Her hair was twisted up off her neck and she was dressed in a suit, but she'd undergone a soft, subtle change since they'd become lovers. Was he the only one who saw that sweet sexiness about her?

"What are you doing down this way?"

"It's been a fantastic day." She shoved a newspaper into his hand and pointed to an article. "Look. Read it aloud. I want to hear the words."

Aaron stared at the headline and slowly read. "'Harrington Resort Tops the A-list of Favored Florida Keys Escapes.'"

"Keep reading."

"I'll get it wet and something tells me you can already recite it word for word." He handed her the paper. "How about the *Reader's Digest* version?"

She took the paper and held it up like a trophy. "It says that I top the list. Food. Accommodations. Entertainment. Says we're pricey, but if that's the only negative, I'm in heaven. Edward's going to be impressed."

He grinned and gave her a hug. "Congrats. That's quite an accomplishment given the competition moving in down here." He picked up the day's receipts off the desk and stuffed them into the folder for Rosa.

She hesitated. "I keep meaning to ask. Why don't you have a computer? It'd make keeping track of the business so much easier. In today's world, it's ridiculous to keep books by hand."

He swallowed. "Look, Charlie. No offense, but I don't tell you how to run your hotel."

"But it would be easier with a computer."

Aaron leaned forward so their faces were close enough to kiss, but that wasn't his mood. "I'm not as inept as you think. I know what's coming in and what's going out. As long as the first is bigger than the second and the bank says I have close to what the difference is, I don't give it much thought."

He reached for a cigarette and then put it down. He was trying to quit. He couldn't tell her he'd never touched a computer. He paid Rosa to help him keep things in balance, but no way he wanted Charlie to know what a moron he was. Damned if he'd give her any more reason to look down on him.

"It was just a suggestion," she said.

"It's my freaking business. I don't answer to Edward Harrington and I damn sure don't have to answer to his granddaughter." He picked up the hose and twisted it on, ending the conversation, but he could feel the claws of a trap closing around him.

Charlie stood and stared at him a minute then stormed off toward the bungalow.

The boat was immaculate by the time Aaron calmed down enough to realize he'd already been over the same section three times. What was he upset about? He wasn't stupid. Uneducated maybe, but he didn't have to stand by and let Charlie chip away at him. He might not have had much going into this relationship, but he'd had his self-respect. And that was one thing he intended to keep, even if it meant Charlie hated him.

He rolled up the hose and glared at the bright red Harrington logo on the side of Charlie's hotel. All of a sudden spending an evening with her sounded like torture. He changed into dry clothes and headed for the Gecko.

Straddling his regular stool, he asked Raul to draw him a beer. He reached behind the bar and picked up the phone. Hopefully Zelda was still at her desk and he could leave a message for his prying wife.

Charlie answered. "Harrington's. May I help you?"

This was not his day. "I'm grabbing dinner at the Gecko. Don't wait up." Without waiting for her response, he clicked the phone off.

Raul returned from serving another customer and drummed his fingers on the bar. "*Una problema* in paradise?"

"Paradise is full of Venus flytraps."

Raul shot him that stupid know-it-all bartender grin. "*Venus* and *trap* being the key words here."

Aaron ignored him and took a swig of beer, feeling very much like the fly.

Chapter Twelve

The Budweiser clock behind the bar read midnight as Aaron made his way out of the Gecko, still undecided whether to go home or crash on the boat. Home? When had he started thinking of Charlie's bungalow as home? This whole bogus marriage wasn't turning out like he'd planned. Things would have been simpler if Charlie were actually the uptight snob he'd expected. Then what she thought of him wouldn't matter.

As he passed the dock, he glanced toward the *Free Wind* and stopped dead. A dark figure crept across the deck.

Careful to keep in the shadows of the other boats, Aaron eased toward the gangplank. The intruder jiggled the office doorknob.

Aaron clenched his right fist and stole up behind him. He grabbed the guy's arm, spun him, and slammed him against the door. "Thurman!"

Perry flattened himself against the wood, staring at Aaron's fist.

Aaron fought the temptation to lay him out on the deck. "What the hell are you doing on my boat?" Never taking his eyes off him, he slowly released his hold.

Shrinking away from Aaron's fist, Perry straightened his suit jacket. "I thought it was about time you and I became friends. I mean, we both care for Charlotte and we really should get along."

"At midnight?" He willed his fingers to unclench. "You board my boat uninvited again and I'll have you arrested for trespassing."

Thurman moved to the gangplank. He stood there a second, then turned and left the boat without responding.

Aaron checked to make sure the boat was secure. The cabin door was still locked and the office seemed untouched. What had Thurman been looking for? He let out a breath, thankful he'd had the foresight to store his copy of the pre-nuptial agreement in Raul's safe at the Gecko..

Pacing around the boat, he debated whether to call the cops. But what could they do? No doubt Thurman was watching and waiting for him to leave the boat unattended again. He wouldn't put it past him to try and sabotage the boat. That answered one question. Tonight he'd sleep here.

CHARLOTTE COULDN'T SLEEP. Aaron hadn't come home tonight. Why was he so angry? She'd just been trying to help. She was beginning to think he ran his business the same way he lived his life, by the seat of his khaki shorts. Up until their so-called marriage, she'd pegged him as a playboy, plain and simple. But now, she found she'd married a chameleon. He could switch from carefree ladies' man to temperamental and brooding with no warning.

She rolled over and frowned at the clock—2:00 a.m. Why was she lying here worrying about it? If she couldn't sleep, why should her exasperating husband be allowed to?

Without the benefit of a moon, the night shrouded the dock in murkiness. The deck creaked as she stepped on board the *Free Wind* and approached the shadowed door that led to Aaron's cuddy below. An icy chill ran down her spine and she glanced behind her.

Huge hands grabbed her shoulders and slammed her against the wall. Her heart jammed into her throat and refused to beat. She froze, staring at Aaron's menacing countenance and his drawn back fist.

Seconds ticked by like eternity. She couldn't breathe. Finally, his features relaxed. His fist unclenched and his fingers trembled as he explored her face. "Baby, don't ever sneak up on me like that," he whispered, dragging her close. "You scared the hell out of me."

She scared him? Charlotte wound her arms around his waist and waited for his breathing to steady. Or was that hers?

"Next time, say something. I could have—" His heart pounded against her chest and he held her so tight she fought to breathe.

"Aaron, what's wrong? Who did you think I was?"

He backed up and ran his hands through his hair. "I found Thurman snooping around the boat a couple hours ago."

"Perry? What was he—?" She didn't wait for Aaron to answer, but continued thinking out loud. The loan document wasn't enough. "He's looking for proof that the marriage is a farce to discredit me."

"Is this typical for him or is it more personal?"

She scrubbed her eyes. "All the Thurman men are at the top of their profession. His father's a renowned plastic surgeon. His oldest brother started his own software company. The other is raking in a fortune as a New York stockbroker."

"And Perry's still working his way to the top," Aaron added.

"Perry's the youngest. He planned years ago to accelerate his climb up the corporate ladder at Harrington Resorts by marrying me and manipulating his way into Edward's good graces. I figured out his scheme, but not before I'd sung his praises to my grandfather."

He shrugged. "So tell Edward what an ass Perry is and be done with it."

"Edward believes that women allow emotions to dictate their decisions. If I admit how much of a fool Perry made of me, it just confirms his opinion. We both lose. He might fire Perry, but it would destroy what little confidence he has in me. Everything I've worked for would be for nothing."

"I don't get it. You're killing yourself to do the old man a favor. Why don't you just tell him the way it is and see what happens? What's the worst he can do, fire you? He needs you now more than you need him. There are plenty of other resorts that would trip all over each other to hire you."

"I can't." Her breath caught in her throat. "I spent my childhood following Edward around, dreaming of being just like him when I grew up. He'd brag to everyone that I was a chip off the old block. I guess he never took me seriously, but I took every word he said to heart." She blinked back tears. "I have to prove I can do this, not only to Edward, but to myself."

Adrenaline dissipated and Charlotte trembled. Her body sagged against the wall, suddenly bone tired. Aaron wrapped her in his arms, but she couldn't stop shaking. She'd never felt so worn down. There had to be some concrete evidence to ruin Perry.

AT 5:00 P.M. CHARLOTTE TREKKED up to the Crow's Nest, the Harrington's rooftop bar, to see if the *Free Wind* had returned to port. With the storm brewing, maybe Aaron would come in early. The wind tossed her hair back and the air was fresh with the smell of rain. Heavy clouds rumbled across the sky from the west, but Aaron's slip was empty.

She squinted to see if any boats were coming in, but visibility was limited with the drizzle. She got back into the elevator and tried to put the storm out of her mind. If there was one thing Aaron was good at, it was handling that boat. Well, okay, so he was good at a few other things, too.

By seven, she was back in the Crow's Nest for the fourth time, scanning the churning sea with more trepidation than she cared to admit. Dark clouds hung overhead, heavy and oppressive. It seemed the storm had settled in for the night. The open-air tables sat wet and deserted. No one with any sense would be on the roof in this weather. As a blinding flash of lightning illuminated the clouds, she shuddered at the thought of Aaron caught in this.

Was the *Free Wind* out there among the churning white-caps? She wrapped her arms around her chest and listened to the thunder tumble across the island. Her heart was in her throat. Was this what parents went through when their children stayed out past curfew? Not that her parents would have been home to worry even if she had given them reason.

AARON WIPED THE RAIN OUT of his eyes as he helped the last of the passengers unload their equipment. He turned and stumbled back against the rail as Charlie launched herself into his arms.

"What are you doing out in this mess?" he asked, pushing a lock of wet hair off her face.

"I was worried about you."

"Really?" He could feel her heart racing and she was ice-cold. He covered her lips in a warm kiss then gave her a hug and pointed her toward the cuddy. "It'll only take a minute to finish up here. Why don't you wait below?"

She darted below deck while he checked to make sure no one had left anything behind. He hooked up the electricity to the boat, grabbed the cash box, and locked the office.

Cautioning himself not to read too much into Charlie's pale face and wide brown eyes, he deliberately slowed his pace down the steps. She was frightened of storms. It's not like she was afraid of losing him.

She looked so helpless and bedraggled shivering at his tiny galley table. The French twist she'd meticulously woven her hair into was soaked and falling down. The rain had altered her conservative yellow dress into a sexy, sheer scrap. The thin fabric outlined every detail of her undergarments, right down to the lace design on her slip.

When she looked up at him, his defenses melted. Her liquid brown eyes reflected more than fear. He dropped to his knees in front of her and held her tight. No woman had ever made him feel like a hero. He ran his hands down her back and soothed her trembling body. The air steamed.

She shuddered then slowly relaxed beneath his touch. He was in control, right up until the small sigh escaped her lips.

Control, hell! Gathering her into his arms, he captured her trembling lips and tumbled them onto the berth. He shoved the soggy yellow dress up to her waist and squeezed her bottom. "How do you get this thing off?"

Charlie sat up and peeled the dress over her head. She brought her lips back to his and wiggled out of her underwear faster than he could get out of his shorts and search for protection. He rolled her over until he was on top and pushed his knee between her thighs. He placed the pillow beneath her head, then filled his hands with her breasts.

God, she fit him so good. He didn't want to think about how much this woman turned him on. Of all the women he'd made love to, he'd never experienced anything like Charlie.

He pulled the sheet over them and she snuggled against his chest. Maybe they should talk about why they were together before he started believing this was real. "Work go okay today?"

"Things were pretty calm, except my morning chef missed work for the second time this week." Her body stiffened. "And Edward called right in the middle of us scrambling to get breakfast out."

"Why do you let your grandfather control you?" He could not figure out why someone as strong as Charlie would let anyone manipulate her into this situation.

"I love him. I've always wanted to make him proud. He's really a sweetheart."

"Right. A sweetheart with a control freak personality!"

She rubbed her cheek against his chest. "Yeah, but he single-handedly made Harrington Resorts a successful five-star chain and he did it from the ground up."

"What do you mean single-handedly? The man barks and an entire army jumps."

"Employees, not family. He pays them to jump. Grandmother never worked. He bought the Marathon Key resort for my dad, but Daddy played at working like he did everything else and spent his energy keeping Mom entertained. Edward vehemently disapproves of Don's lifestyle, but he continues to support him."

"He supports everyone because it gives him power over them." Aaron raised one eyebrow. "And you don't strike me as the type who likes to be told what to do."

She ran one finger around his nipple. "Guilty. But, there is something innately wrong about one member of the family working so hard to support everyone else's habits. I mean, nobody made him take care of everyone. I admire him for that."

"Did you ask him about his heart condition?"

Charlotte closed her eyes. "I considered it, but the phone just didn't seem like the right way to discuss something that serious. Too easy for him to avoid the subject. Besides, he wasn't exactly in a congenial mood."

"Perry feeding him crap again?"

"They are talking daily. Edward knew about the loan." She twisted the sheet between her fingers. "Aaron, if we don't find something on Perry fast, Edward is going to promote him to an executive position and I'll be answering to the jerk."

"Did you call Monte Carlo again?"

She shrugged. "I've left three messages, but the only person I know is the manager and he's on vacation. His assistant said he'd have him call me if he talked to him, but nothing yet."

Charlie curled up like an exhausted kitten against his chest and her eyes drifted closed.

Aaron propped up in bed and held her, lost in the sound of the thunder and the rain pelting the windows. This storm outside would end, but what about the one brewing inside him?

He wrapped a strand of her hair around his finger. What had begun as a mutually beneficial business arrangement had turned into something...more. They'd started out to save both their businesses, but now he couldn't walk away until he knew Charlie and her empire were safe from Perry Thurman's clutches.

Charlie hadn't said anything about Boston, but they both knew that's how this would end. Charlie had no choice now. Whichever way things played out, she'd either be in Boston running things or she'd be there trying to protect the business from Thurman.

And there was no place for him in Massachusetts.

His stomach growled and he grabbed his watch off the table. Ten o'clock. Geez, no wonder. He hadn't eaten since lunch.

Charlie stretched and arched her back. "I'm hungry."

"You should get back to the bungalow." He eased her out of his arms.

"Aren't you coming?"

He fought to divert his eyes from her breasts as she sat up and the sheet slid to her waist. If he was going to get out of this marriage without it killing him, he couldn't sleep with her every night. He had to put distance between them. "I think I'll stay here tonight."

Escaping the confusion in Charlie's eyes, he left her below to dress. He went on deck and took a long drag on the first cigarette he'd had all day. It was stupid to allow her here after the incident the other night. She had no idea how vulnerable she was. Vulnerable to Perry and his underhandedness. Vulnerable to her grandfather's whims. And worst of all, vulnerable to Aaron and this relationship.

The best thing he could do was to make a clean break and end this marriage before it consumed both of them. But he couldn't walk away yet. They'd made a deal. A deal he'd been well compensated for.

The sooner they proved Thurman was up to no good and set her grandfather straight, the sooner he could bail out of her life and move on. Thurman would be history. Charlie'd move to Boston and he could get back to his old life.

Still, none of that solved the melancholy mood that had him in its grip tonight. He listened to the rain dripping off the cover. If he started sleeping on the boat, that would give Perry more ammunition to carry back to old man Harrington. If he stayed at the bungalow, might as well hang a flashing welcome sign for Percy to snoop around the *Free Wind*. The guy had already made one suspicious midnight visit. Aaron wasn't sure what he was up to, but it couldn't be good. Just what he needed was for Thurman to sabotage the boat.

Plus, the bungalow meant sharing a bed with Charlie, and as appealing as that was, it led to more involvement. God, it was going to hurt to watch her pack up and leave.

He heard her come upstairs onto the deck, but kept his back to her. Maybe if he ignored her, she'd go back to the bungalow.

She didn't.

It took all his control to wait her out, but he didn't say a word. Finally she walked off the boat.

He took one last drag off the cigarette and ground it out.

He hadn't taken more than three puffs off the thing. Charlie was the reason he'd been trying to quit and the reason he couldn't all rolled into one frustrating woman.

Chapter Thirteen

Aaron stepped into the Gecko, skimming water from his arms. It had rained every afternoon this week. The bar was bustling with people searching for inside entertainment to pass the time. He took the last available stool and snared the frosty mug of beer Raul slid his way. "Early crowd today."

"They started filing in about an hour ago when the first shower blew over. Tropical rain's good for business."

Aaron took a long swig from his beer. "Yours, maybe. It's beginning to thin out in my end of the world. Between the boat being out of the water almost three weeks and now this rain, my busy season ain't so busy."

"Yeah, well you've got *mucho dinero* now. Why worry?"

"Thanks, pal. You make me sound like a kept man."

"Well, Casanova, you haven't taken another woman home since your marriage." Raul handed the guy next to Aaron another drink and flashed his white teeth. "Doesn't sound like such a bad gig to me. Classy *senora*, loads of money, renovated boat."

Raul seemed intent on getting under his skin. It was working. "All temporary, my friend. All temporary."

He glanced around the room. Hardly a vacant seat in the house. Two guys were sitting at the end of the bar. One was a regular, but the other seemed out of place. Could have something to do with his foreign accent. French maybe? He looked vaguely familiar.

The band cranked up in the corner and filled the room with reggae. Not bad. Better than the classical stuff Charlie listened to around the bungalow. A redhead hovering close to the Frenchman winked at Aaron. He narrowed his eyes and continued to scan the crowd.

The redhead didn't waste time making her way over. She wiggled her scantily clad butt in between him and the guy on the next stool and made sure to rub her breasts against his arm in the process. Her thin T-shirt barely covered her large nipples.

Did every bar come equipped with a woman like her? Did barkeeps order them out of a catalog like furniture or glasses? Over thirty, but still trying to look twenty. Her skirt was wider than it was long and the shirt didn't come anywhere close to meeting the waistband. He narrowed his eyes at her hand resting on his thigh and cringed at the thought of those bloodred claws coming anywhere close to a certain part of his anatomy.

She motioned to Raul and pressed against Aaron's leg. "Can I buy you a drink?"

Aaron held up the glass Raul had luckily just refilled. "I'm fine."

She leaned forward, her shirt falling away and presenting him a full view of her breasts. Didn't even have to look close to tell they were implants. As boob jobs went, this one wasn't even good. He saw her mouth open and was tempted to say her next line for her.

"Then buy me a drink."

He handed Raul enough money to cover his drinks and hers. "Pour the lady whatever she wants. Time I got home to my wife."

Aaron grabbed the phone from behind the bar and dialed Charlie's office. She was working late again so he volunteered to stop by the grocery and cook dinner.

Standing under the Gecko overhang, Aaron rubbed his eyes. He'd had a thousand girls like that redhead, but he'd never realized how predictable and boring they were.

CHARLOTTE STOPPED ON THE FRONT porch of the bungalow and shook the water off her umbrella. If this rain didn't stop soon they were all going to grow webbed feet. She opened the door, looking forward to a relaxing dinner of boiled shrimp. Every woman should come home to a husband with Aaron's culinary skills.

But the bungalow was empty. No lights, no welcoming aroma, and no Aaron. Strange. He'd called an hour ago. The man needed a cell phone, but every time she suggested it he argued that he would not be tied to a damn phone 24/7.

She changed into a pair of sweats and a T-shirt, but still no sign of her husband. Switching on the TV for company, she reminded herself to be patient. Aaron did not operate on a time clock.

The gray sky turned to inky-black as night moved in and Charlotte paced. Sitting down at her laptop, she surfed the Net looking at cell phones for Aaron. He couldn't complain as long as she was paying for it, could he? Okay, he could. But she needed to be able to get in touch with him. Maybe she should call the Gecko. But he'd said he was leaving when he called.

She poured a glass of wine and sat down on the sofa, but the TV didn't offer one channel that could hold her interest.

The phone rang and she grabbed it before the second ring.

"Is this Charlotte Brody?"

"Yes." Cold chills ran down her spine at the cold tone.

"Ma'am, this is Officer Perez calling from the hospital emergency room. There's been an incident on your husband's boat."

Sitting up straight, she suddenly focused on the officer's words. "Emergency room? Is Aaron okay?"

The officer's voice remained calm. "Your husband is going to be okay. But you might want to come down here."

Oh, God. She covered her mouth to keep from screaming into the phone. "How bad is he hurt?"

"Ma'am, I'm not a doctor. But his injuries are not life threatening. We can fill you in when you get here."

"I'm on my way." Charlotte shoved her feet into her sneakers and grabbed a sweatshirt. Where the hell was her purse? Before Aaron moved in, the bungalow had always been immaculate. Everything in its place. But she'd gotten as lax as he was about leaving things where they landed.

Spotting her purse on the chair, she grabbed it and dug her keys out, already darting for the car.

The roads were slick, but luckily it wasn't far to the hospital. Not only was she not sure if she locked the car, she wasn't even positive she shut the door as she raced up to the emergency room counter. "Aaron Brody, please. I'm his wife."

Could the woman type any slower? "Brody with a *Y?*"

"Yes." Oh, come on. This wasn't New York or some huge city. There were only two other people in the waiting room.

A police officer came through the door and nodded toward her. "Mrs. Brody?"

"Yes. Where's my husband?"

"They're stitching him up right now. It'll just be a few minutes."

Charlotte followed him to a chair. "What happened? Did somebody attack him?"

The officer's weathered face revealed nothing. "We haven't gotten a full statement. We left a team to secure the site and brought Mr. Brody here for treatment. Apparently he surprised two intruders on his boat. There was a scuffle and Mr. Brody sustained a stab wound to his left arm."

Charlotte rubbed her hands up and down the chill bumps on her own arms.

Perry was behind this. After being caught once, she doubted he'd come on board again. But he wasn't above hiring someone. "Did you catch them?"

"No," the officer said.

She'd brought this on Aaron. If not for her, Perry wouldn't even know Aaron existed.

The receptionist approached. "Mr. Brody is ready for visitors, as soon as you're done here."

The woman's rubber soles squeaked as she led them down the sterile hallway. The officer stood back and let Charlotte approach the bed alone. Aaron sat propped against the pillows, wearing no shirt and a white bandage around his upper arm. Her hungry eyes surveyed every inch of him, searching for any damage. Other than a split lip and a purple bruise spreading across his left cheekbone, he looked wonderful. Her hand trembled as she ran her palm down his cheek. Tears sprang to her eyes before she could stop them.

Aaron covered her hand with his and brought it to his lips. "I'm okay, Charlie."

"I kept waiting for you to come home, but I had no idea."

"I was on the way to the grocery store. But after Tuesday night I decided to swing by and make sure the boat was secure."

"What happened Tuesday night?" the officer asked, moving a chair up for Charlotte.

She sat on the edge of the bed and motioned him into the chair.

"Similar situation. I left the Gecko around midnight and headed home. As I passed the *Free Wind,* I caught someone snooping around."

The officer opened his notebook. "Did you file a report?"

"I didn't file a report because I know the SOB," Aaron said, glancing at Charlie.

She shook her head and rubbed her eyes. "You don't think

Perry was one of the guys tonight though, right? He's not the physical type."

The officer looked at Charlotte. "Perry who, ma'am? Do you believe he's the one responsible for this?"

She stared at Aaron, then finally turned to the officer. "Perry Thurman. He had to be behind it."

The policeman looked from Charlotte to Aaron. "So does Perry Thurman have an ax to grind with you?"

"He's been causing problems for my wife." Aaron nodded at Charlotte. "She runs the Harrington Resort and Thurman wants her job. That's the facts, unless you want me to speculate."

The officer took more notes. "And how does Tuesday tie to the incident tonight?"

Aaron rubbed his forehead. "Thurman was searching the boat the other night. I told him that if he showed up again, I'd have him charged with trespassing. So I've slept on the boat a couple nights to keep an eye out. I figure Thurman for mind games. Looking for anything to hurt Charlie and accelerate his climb up the corporate ladder, but nothing physical."

"I'm the one he's after." Charlotte squeezed Aaron's hand. "I'm sure Perry hired those guys."

"Yeah, and since the police didn't catch them, that'll be a bitch to prove," Aaron said.

"Can you tell me exactly what happened tonight?"

Aaron took a deep breath. "I walked by the boat. Saw movement. A guy dressed in dark clothes trying to break into my office. He kicked the door in, but I grabbed his arms and pinned them back. He had a black knit cap over his face and I couldn't turn loose of his arms long enough to yank it off. He kicked backward and caught my shin. I started to spin him when a second guy caught me from behind and pulled me off the first one. We scuffled and I kicked the first guy in the groin. He went down, but the other guy had me in a choke hold."

"They both had on masks?"

"Yeah. We circled each other and exchanged a couple blows. I had him against the rail when the first guy came at me with a knife. I shoved one guy overboard, but the one with the knife evidently took the pain in his groin personal. He jumped at me cursing in Spanish."

"Can you describe him?"

"Small. Wiry build. Fluent in street Spanish."

The officer continued writing. "And did he go into the water also?"

Aaron shook his head. "No. We fought it out, but I couldn't get the knife away from him. He kept slicing it back and forth to keep me at a distance. I lunged for it and he stabbed for my chest, but I turned and the knife caught my arm instead. I was so pissed, I chased him down the dock."

"Did they take anything?"

"Not that I could find. I must have surprised them shortly after they boarded because the cuddy was still locked."

The hospital finally released Aaron around ten, but before he'd let Charlotte take him home, he insisted she drive by the boat.

Two officers were still on board. Yellow crime scene tape surrounded the *Free Wind* and one officer stood watch. The second had a flashlight in his hand shining it down the side of the hull.

When she and Aaron tried to board, the officer blocked the way. "Crime scene, sir. You can't come aboard."

"It's my boat," Aaron said.

The officer demanded identification, then moved aside and allowed them to cross the short gangplank.

She followed as Aaron checked the cuddy and the office. Nothing out of place, so that was good. He'd have to get someone to replace the office door tomorrow morning.

They drove the remaining distance to the bungalow in silence.

When Aaron crawled into bed his forehead was creased and his lips were a thin line.

"What do you think Perry's planning?" she asked.

Aaron stretched out and rubbed his arm. "Not sure. But I need to know every detail about what happened between you and Thurman."

"You mean back in college?"

"I mean everything leading up to tonight."

"What are we going to gain by talking about this?" Charlotte scrubbed her hands over her eyes.

"I need the facts to be able to deal with him."

God, she did not want to dredge up all the old hurt. She took a deep breath. "Perry was the first guy to show an interest in me, romantically I mean. I was twenty-three and had never had more than a couple dates with the same guy."

She sat up and drew her knees under her chin. This was too personal. She didn't want Aaron to know what a loser she was. She squeezed her eyes shut.

He touched her arm. "Charlie, you can talk to me. We're in this together."

She swallowed and opened her eyes, staring into Aaron's concerned expression. He needed to understand. "Perry was so charming. When he asked me out, I was flattered. The only guys that ever talked to me usually wanted help with an assignment."

Aaron turned and propped his head up on his good arm. "Go on."

"He told me he loved me, wanted to marry me. We talked about the future, running our own chain of hotels. We started sleeping together."

Tears swamped her eyes, but she had to finish. She was the woman who never cried, yet tonight the emotions were raw. "He was the first, you know?"

He reached out and ran the back of his knuckles down her cheek. "I hate to put you through this."

"I couldn't wait to introduce him to Edward. They hit it off, like I knew they would. Everything was perfect, until I let myself into his apartment one afternoon." She took a deep breath and welcomed the warmth of Aaron's arms. "I guess he figured it was his roommate, because he didn't get out of bed. I recognized a female voice. He was having sex with another woman on the sheets I'd bought for us."

She could picture everything as vividly as if she were standing in that apartment. Her voice cracked. "She said she didn't know how he could stand to have sex with someone as homely as me. He laughed and said—"

Aaron touched one finger to her lips. "Don't say any more. I get the picture. I'm going to kill the bastard."

As humiliating as it was, now that she'd opened the emotional floodgates, she couldn't stop. "They joked about how stupid I was. He said he'd stay married to me long enough to take over Harrington's and then they'd have it made. By the time I figured out what was happening, there wouldn't be anything I could do."

Aaron held her cradled in his arms, but he didn't speak.

"I was mortified. I wanted to slink out of the apartment and pretend I hadn't heard them. But my pride wouldn't let me. When I opened the bedroom door, he jumped out of bed and tried to tell me it was nothing. I felt like such an idiot." She swiped at her damn tears. "Have you ever noticed that little bump on his otherwise perfect brown nose?"

He laughed. "Good for you."

"Yeah, but I didn't go to Edward." Charlotte eased out of Aaron's arms, got out of bed, and paced. She was too agitated to lay still. "I didn't know it, but Edward and Perry flew to Monte Carlo the next morning. When they returned, Edward told me he'd promised Perry the manager position after we graduated."

"So he got what he wanted, or at least the first step toward it?"

"I should have leveled with Edward then, but Perry had me pegged. He knew I wouldn't make myself look like a fool."

She leaned against the dresser and shook her head. She was finally beginning to calm down. "Perry and I both graduated with a BA, but Edward sent him off to Monte Carlo as a manager. So for two years while Perry realized *my* dream, I did the grunt work at the Boston resort and took classes."

"What did you tell Edward about not getting married?"

"That I needed to finish my master's first and learn the business, then we simply let the marriage idea die."

She paced to the door, spun, and went back to the window. "After I earned my master's, Edward put me here to prove myself. 'Work my way up,' he said. 'No favors for the boss's granddaughter.' The Marathon resort is the oldest in the chain and had been neglected since Daddy's death. But I love this resort."

Aaron walked over and wrapped his arms around her waist, resting his chin on top of her head. "Yeah, well if Perry wants to play dirty, he's come to the right guy."

Chapter Fourteen

Aaron wanted to lure Thurman into a dark alley and beat the crap out of him, but for Charlie's sake, he'd settle for exposing him. He had to prove that Thurman was behind the goons who broke into the boat.

Not wanting to tip the guy off, he'd talked the police out of questioning him, for the time being. He had another plan. However, there was some consolation that the name Perry Thurman was now officially on a police report.

The boat was still taped off and Aaron wasn't supposed to get his arm wet for a week. He canceled his tour and made an appointment for a guy to come repair the office door.

Charlie invited him to stop by for lunch after he finished at the *Free Wind*. The resort seemed a good place to start his own snooping. He could play that game as well as Thurman could.

He grabbed two turkey sandwiches from the corner deli and headed to Charlie's office.

"Well," she asked when he opened the door. "Did they find anything?"

"No unknown prints. Which figures since they were wearing gloves." Aaron watched Charlie clear a space on her desk for the sandwiches. "As far as I can tell, I arrived before they got into anything."

"Perry is acting smug. Even on the off chance he wasn't behind it, he had to have noticed the police scouring your boat, but he didn't say a word."

"Cops promised to keep an eye on him. But I'm going to sleep on the boat from here on."

"Hire somebody. I don't want you down there alone. Not after this."

"I'm a big boy, Charlie. While Thurman was in prep school, I was surviving the streets of South Miami." He winked. "Could you have security watch Thurman without him finding out? See if they can catch him talking to anyone suspicious."

"Sure." She rubbed her thumb over his bruised cheek then dug a bag out from under her desk. "I got you something that might come in handy."

He took the bag and pulled out a cell phone. "I thought we'd discussed this."

"It'll make me feel better."

"You're right. It'd be good if we could get hold of each other." He'd never wanted a cell phone, but given the circumstances. "Thanks."

They finished their sandwiches and he decided to head for the Gecko. Raul should be opening up about now. But first he walked through the resort restaurant. He had a hunch about where he'd heard that French accent. He waited until the chef came out of the kitchen. Sure enough, it was the same guy who had taken to hanging out at the Gecko lately.

THE GECKO WAS QUIET, with only a couple of early patrons. Ceiling fans circulated just enough of a breeze to keep the open-air dive from sweltering.

"What brings you in this early? Figured you'd still be basking in the sparkling blue of the Atlantic." Raul stopped short at the sight of Aaron's face. "What the hell happened to you?"

Aaron gave the other two regulars a quick once-over and dismissed them as harmless. "Two guys broke into the boat last night."

"Dios!" Raul frowned.

"I'm after Thurman's ass." Aaron blew out a breath. "Do you remember that Frenchman who was in here the other night? He and another guy were tossing back beers at the end of the bar."

"Older guy?"

Aaron nodded. "Yeah, drinking with a young Latino."

"Sal, a local fisherman. They've been in here together two or three nights a week for the last month. The Frenchman can put it away. I don't know how Sal can afford it."

"Sal always picks up the tab?"

Raul's eyes narrowed. "I don't remember the Frenchman ever pulling out his wallet."

"Don't you think that's odd? Why would Sal always be buying another guy drinks?"

"Sal's married to Rosa's cousin, two or three times removed. He's got a wife and umpteen kids living in a falling down rattrap outside of town. She'd skin him if she knew he was throwing away money on that fancy gigolo."

Aaron smiled. "That was my first thought. The Frenchman is Charlie's chef. He was ogling a cute little brunette waitress at lunch. My guess is Thurman's funding these little drinking escapades to make sure the chef's too hungover to show up for the early shift."

"Thurman's the guy that Charlotte didn't want to marry bad enough to pay you a hundred grand?"

"Yep." He jotted down his new cell number on a napkin and handed it to Raul. "If Sal shows up, let me know. I'd like to have a little chat with him."

"A cell phone?" Raul grinned.

"I'm not sure how far Thurman will go to prove our marriage is a farce. I don't want her hurt."

Raul flashed that know-it-all bartender look that made the hair on the back of Aaron's neck stand on end. "Is it a farce, my friend? You're sure getting drawn into the lady's problems."

"Charlie doesn't realize how ruthless this guy is." Aaron stood and dropped a couple bills on the bar. "Up until last night it was mind games. Thurman just upped the stakes."

AARON STOPPED BY THE DIVE shop to arrange for one of the guys to help on the boat for the next couple days until his arm healed. Not being able to get in the water stunk.

His cell phone startled him when it chimed "Reveille." He had to figure out what he did to get that damn ring tone.

Raul was on the other end. "They're here."

On the way to the bar, Aaron called Charlie's office. "I'm going to grab dinner at the Gecko and sleep on the *Free Wind* tonight."

"Aaron, please be careful."

"I'm always careful."

He walked into the Gecko and spotted Sal and the Frenchman laughing at a small table at the far end of the room. Judging by the bottles on the table, they were on at least round two. Aaron ordered a whiskey and waited. The drunker Sal was when he confronted him the looser his tongue might be.

The club slowly came alive with night sounds, but Aaron continued to nurse the same drink. The band of the evening arrived with spiked hair and leather. He figured they weren't old enough to be allowed out past midnight, so maybe he wouldn't have to listen to too much of their noise. Sal and the Frenchman continued to put away the booze. The Frenchman drank two to Sal's one.

Aaron ordered dinner and kept one eye on the odd couple. It was closing in on midnight when the Frenchman stood up and stumbled toward the men's room for the fifth time.

Aaron maneuvered his way to Sal's table and sat down. "Sal, isn't it?"

"Do I know you?" Sal squinted through bloodshot eyes.

"Aaron Brody."

"Oh, *sí,* the *Free Wind* guy."

He nodded. "Who's the fancy pants?"

Sparks lit Sal's dark eyes. "*Qué el infierno?* I no hang with no fancy pants."

Aaron stood as he saw the Frenchman staggering their way. "Looks pretty fancy to me, pal."

He didn't have long to wait until the odd couple weaved their way out of the bar. He handed Raul a couple bills to cover his tab and stopped to see which way they went. Just as he expected, they headed in opposite directions.

Aaron followed Sal at a distance. The guy finally stepped into a phone booth, placed a call, and then made a beeline down the wharf. He moved pretty fast for a guy who'd consumed five beers.

"I'll be damned," Aaron muttered when Thurman stepped out of the shadows. He and Sal exchanged a few words, Sal handed Thurman a piece of paper, probably the tab from the Gecko, and Thurman greased Sal's palm with a sizeable number of bills.

He waited until they were out of earshot and called Raul. "He met Thurman all right. Don't think Sal cares much for me. Can you find out what kind of deal they've got cooking?"

"I'll give it a shot. Don't do anything stupid."

"Yeah," Aaron commented. "Hey, listen, I'm sleeping on the boat tonight, so if you see smoke, send out the posse."

CHARLOTTE JUMPED AND SAT straight up in bed. The phone rang a second time and she grabbed the receiver. "Aaron?"

"Funny, that's who I was looking for," a bubbly female voice said. "He was supposed to be here an hour ago."

"Who is this?"

The phone clicked off.

Charlotte got up and paced across the room, spun, and glared at the offending phone. Her throat went dry. She didn't recognize the voice and didn't want to believe Aaron might be meeting another woman. She'd thought… What had she thought? That just because they'd become lovers that it meant something to Aaron? That he cared? She of all people should know better.

There was barely enough light to make her way to the kitchen and she stumbled over a pair of Aaron's sneakers in the hall. She growled as she kicked them out of her way.

She grabbed a bottle of water out of the fridge and twisted the cap off. If he were seeing someone else, why would he give the woman this number? The man wasn't stupid.

She gulped down the water and practiced breathing. Her heart thudded so fast she worried it might jump out of her chest. Aaron's affairs were nothing to her. It was just a stupid phone call. She wouldn't act like some ticked off, jealous wife. She climbed back into bed, but sleep was impossible.

Charlotte tossed until the sheets were in knots. She worried about Aaron sleeping on that deserted boat. She worried more that he might be sleeping with some other woman. She… she…she simply worried.

A LARGE TOUR ARRIVED PROMPTLY at three. At five minutes after, Charlotte's phone rang. She rushed to the front desk to try and calm a furious tour director who had booked twenty-seven rooms and arrived to find only twenty-three available.

As Charlotte was calling another resort to see if they could accommodate the other guests, Perry stepped up and took the tour director's hand. "Ms. O'Connor, isn't it? What seems to be the problem?"

Before Charlotte could close her gaping mouth, he offered

the entire group a voucher for free dinner in the resort with complimentary drinks and dessert if they'd give them a few minutes to straighten out the issue.

Charlotte finally managed to accommodate the entire group at Harrington's. She'd have to explain to the other guests that there'd been a mix-up and they'd be spending their first night at another hotel. That should go over well.

Ms. O'Connor took the room keys, smiled, and thanked Perry profusely for his special care. She shook her head in disgust at Charlotte and followed the bellboy into the elevator.

Perry leaned across the front desk, eye level with her chest. "How did you mess up the reservation?"

Charlotte shivered at the dirty feel of his eyes on her body. "Someone cancelled their reservation. I wonder who could've done something like that?" she asked facetiously.

"All I've done since I've been here is solve problems."

She didn't flinch. "Strange thing is, Perry, the problems didn't start until you arrived."

He patted her cheek. "You need me, Charlotte. When are you going to admit it?"

"Get your hand off me," she spat, stepping out of reach.

Perry withdrew his hand as if he'd been scalded and his cunning grin evaporated.

She waited until he walked away, then hurried back to her office, and pulled up the reservation to see if she could tell what had happened. Someone onsite with an employee number of 287519 had altered the reservation at 12:58 p.m.

She called Grace, the office manager, and asked her to look up the employee number. Within five minutes she had Maria Estevez sitting in front of her desk.

"No, ma'am. I didn't do anything with that reservation." Her bottom lip quivered.

"Maybe you made a mistake? That happens."

"No. I didn't even touch that reservation," Maria said.

Charlotte tried to keep her voice calm. "What time did you go to lunch?"

"We were so busy all morning. I didn't take my lunch until twelve forty-five."

"Did you go alone?"

She nodded. "*Sí*. We take separate breaks so there are always two at the desk."

"Did you sign out of the workstation before you left?"

"I thought so. I'm always careful." Maria sniffed. "It won't happen again."

Charlotte stared at the tears threatening to overflow Maria's eyes and felt like an ogre. Was she turning into her grandfather? What a horrible thought.

Taking a deep breath, she leaned forward. "It's okay, Maria. I believe you." She couldn't very well come right out and ask if Perry Thurman was around when she left. "Was there anyone else at the desk besides the other two attendants?"

"There were still guests, but the line had gone down. I don't remember anyone out of the ordinary."

Charlotte accompanied Maria back to the desk and asked the other two attendants if they'd noticed anyone lurking about. They assured her they never left the counter unattended and neither had seen a soul behind the desk who could have changed the reservation.

She needed to talk through this with someone. Aaron would have a fresh perspective. When had she started to rely so much on his judgment?

AARON YANKED OFF HIS WET T-shirt, shucked his swim trunks, and stepped into a pair of faded cutoffs. He grabbed a wild Hawaiian shirt he'd bought at a Jimmy Buffet concert in Key West last summer, popped a painkiller for his aching arm, and headed topside. The storm was moving in fast. The cloud of sand blowing across the beach had sun-baked tourists gathering up their paraphernalia and darting for cover. The sooner he finished securing the boat, the sooner he could track Charlie down. He wanted to see her face when he told her about Perry arranging to get her chef plastered.

As he wiped the sand out of his eyes and started cleaning up, Charlie came aboard. He grinned at her baggy khaki slacks and bright orange blouse. She wore little strappy sandals with matching orange beads and a thick French braid hung down her back.

"Nice shirt," she said, watching him fasten the last button. "Did you go in the water today?"

Granted, he probably should have stayed out for another day, but he'd live. "The cut isn't that serious." He smiled and attempted to change the subject. "You're keeping banker's hours these days."

"I wanted to tell you what happened and see what you think."

"Shoot. Talk while I tie things up before this storm blows in."

She followed him into his office, giving every detail about the reservation being cancelled for some large tour.

Aaron placed the cash in the cashbox and locked it. "And Thurman was behind it?"

"I think he waited until Maria left for lunch, found the computer signed in, and cancelled the reservation so we couldn't trace it to him. Then he could show up and play hero."

Aaron looked up from his desk. "Could be. I know for sure he's paying Sal to get your morning chef drunk. I personally saw him give Sal the money."

"Oohh!" She stomped across the deck, twirled, and came back to stand in the doorway. "So that's why Pierre has called in sick so often. When he does come in, he's late. I've got an ad running for a replacement so I can fire him."

"Why not fire Thurman instead? The Frenchman doesn't have a clue. He just thinks he's found a new best bud."

"I have to think about how to handle this."

"Easy. I tell Sal his meal ticket's about to dry up."

A gust of wind sent Brody's Charters caps tumbling across the deck. Aaron dropped a dive weight on top of the papers and he and Charlie ran to chase the runaway caps. The air was heavy with the musty scent of rain. The first large drops pelted down as he captured the last cap and darted under the canopy with Charlie.

He couldn't resist a quick kiss. "Here, pitch the caps in my office. I'll deal with them later."

She deposited her armful and giggled. "There are some things about your job that are a lot more fun than mine."

God, he loved the sound of her laughter. Amazingly, she didn't seem scared of the storm at all with the boat docked.

"There are a lot of things about my job that are more fun than yours." He eased her down on his lap and wrapped her in his arms. "Especially when you come down to help."

Thunder rumbled across the gray sky and the rain peppered down around them. Amazing how Charlotte felt so safe from the storm. She loved the electricity and the smell of the rain when she had the security of sitting cradled in Aaron's arms.

They were both half-wet from chasing the caps and the damp wind was finishing the job. She snuggled against him, relishing the erotic warmth. The man brought her to life.

Maybe that phone call last night was just a woman from his past?

Aaron slid one hand under the hem of her blouse and pressed it flat against her rumbling belly. "Skip lunch again?"

She covered his hand with hers. "I didn't have time."

"Wait here." He scooted her off his lap. "I'll see what's in the fridge."

A few minutes later, she was munching on a bag of chips and sipping a beer. "Such a big spender." The rain provided a secluded curtain around them. Water dripped off the edge of the canopy, creating an intimate setting for their impromptu picnic.

"First you make fun of my shirt and now you're complaining about the gourmet cuisine. There's no pleasing some women."

"Easier than you think. Maybe you could sleep at the bungalow tonight?"

CHARLOTTE SNUGGLED AGAINST Aaron's bare chest and looked out her bedroom window as the day faded to dusk, still awed at how comfortable she was with this relationship. "What's so fun at the Gecko?"

Her hand pressed against his heart and she listened for any hesitation. "Nothing particular."

She ran the inside of one foot up his calf, trying not to think about that stupid phone call. "You spend a lot of time there."

"My friends are there. Why the sudden interest?"

"No specific reason. Just wondering. I've never frequented bars."

"No! Really?" he kidded. "I'm shocked."

"I know. I'm not exactly the party girl type you're used to hanging out with." Great. Was she stooping to fishing for compliments now?

He rolled to the edge of the bed, stood, and reached for his shorts. "We never did have much dinner. You hungry?"

If she was fishing, Aaron didn't bite. She clenched her teeth and rolled to the other side. Why invite rejection? The man obviously wasn't interested in making their marriage real. This was temporary. He probably couldn't wait to return to his playboy lifestyle. Or maybe he already had.

She watched him fry bacon and scramble eggs, even ate what he set in front of her, but she didn't taste it. She had to remember this pretend relationship was her brainstorm. The plan didn't include falling in love. It certainly didn't include forever. Aaron was nice, he was pleasant, and he was fulfilling his end of the bargain.

Do not fall for this man.

Aaron had barely uttered three words since they'd gotten out of bed. She picked up her plate. "I'll clean up the kitchen."

"Thanks." He placed his plate on the counter by the sink and left the room.

She listened to the shower and wondered if he planned to go to the Gecko. That'd be about par. But, by the time she finished the dishes and turned out the kitchen light, he had parked himself in front of the television.

Fine. I can handle this. If he wanted to watch TV all night, she'd catch up on her reading. They could pretend to be husband and wife just like any other miserable couple.

In a huff, she stalked into the bathroom. Look at this mess! Geez, didn't the man ever put anything away? Furiously, she stashed razor and shaving cream under the cabinet. A wet washcloth, a pair of dirty socks, and navy plaid boxers lay crumpled in a pile in a corner.

This is what living with a man's like? Messy, nerve-racking, pain in the— She grabbed his shirt off the peg on the back of the door and inhaled. Sunscreen. Suddenly weak in the knees she hugged the shirt to her chest and dropped to the side of the tub. Aaron. She closed her eyes and pictured his teasing grin. His green eyes smoldering after a warm kiss. His quick temper. A rush of longing swirled around her like a warm mist.

Carrying the shirt, she peeped into the living room. He looked so sexy just sitting there watching TV. She groaned. He looked sexy washing dishes or wearing sneakers with holes.

The whole thing suddenly wasn't such a mystery. She had fallen totally and unconditionally in love with her husband.

Chapter Fifteen

"What?" Aaron paused. "Hold on a minute. Let me go outside."

Voices, both male and female, laughed in the background. Obviously he was hanging out at the Gecko, as usual. A woman said something about guarding his stool. Charlotte's heart plummeted. She was far from the only woman Aaron had unleashed those lethal charms on. He was there with someone. Probably the girl from the phone call.

She waited for him to get outside.

"Charlie, is that you?"

"It's me," she whispered, suddenly feeling awkward for interrupting his evening.

"What's up?"

"Nothing." What was she supposed to say now? "I just wanted to make sure you were planning to sleep on the boat."

"Yeah, I thought we covered that."

"We did, I just—" Charlotte's thoughts vanished. She couldn't just blurt out that she missed him.

"Are you okay?"

"Sure. I just thought we should touch base."

"Hey, Thurman's paying Sal twice whatever tab he can run up while getting your chef soused. He's making a killing tonight. Might want to make arrangements for tomorrow morning. The guy's already leaning on the table and slurring his drink orders."

"Thanks for the tip." She didn't want Aaron sleeping alone on that boat with Perry's goons lurking about. "Be careful."

"I'll be fine. Sleep tight."

Charlotte grabbed a paperback and crawled in bed. She read a couple of paragraphs before realizing she had no idea what had just happened in the story. Disgusted, she pitched the book on the nightstand, rolled over, and turned the light out. Why was she so restless? Maybe because she was alone at home while Aaron was at the Gecko partying with other women?

THE PHONE JARRED HER OUT of a sound sleep. Charlotte grabbed the receiver and tried to focus on the clock. One o'clock in the morning!

"Hey, baby. Are you coming over tonight?" the sultry female voice asked.

"Who the hell is this?" Charlotte demanded. The caller ID read *Out of Area,* which could mean anything from the next island to an unlisted number.

"Shit! I meant to call the cell," the girl said and disconnected.

Charlotte banged the receiver back into the cradle. "Damn Aaron Brody!"

THE NEXT NIGHT WHEN THE WOMAN called, Charlotte was ready. "Who are you?"

"A friend of your husband's." There was a slight pause. "I think it'd be a waste for Aaron to spend all that sex appeal in one place, don't you?"

Charlotte hung up the receiver, picked it back up, and dialed Aaron's cell phone. She had to know where he was.

"Brody," he answered on the third ring, stifling a yawn.

"Aaron?"

"Charlie?" She heard the mattress give. "What's wrong?"

"You were asleep?" she muttered.

"It's one o'clock in the morning. Where else would I be?"

"So you're on the boat?" She suddenly realized her mistake. "I'm sorry. I shouldn't have bothered you." She hung up, but the phone immediately rang.

Aaron didn't even wait for her to say hello. "What the hell's going on?"

"This is the third night a woman has called here looking for you."

He paused. "And you just figured I was sleeping with her?"

"She never calls when you're home."

His tone changed from anger to guarded and cold. "Thanks for the confidence."

Before she could defend herself, he continued. "You get a couple random phone calls and decide I'm in some other woman's bed." She could hear the boat creak. "Hell, I could be at her place right now."

"I… What would you think if you got calls from another man?"

"You think the reason I'm sleeping on the boat is so I can bring another woman here?"

Charlotte took a deep breath, beginning to understand her misjudgment. "No, I know you wouldn't do that."

"Oh, so if I'm on the boat, I'm innocent? But how do you know for sure?" The line hissed when he reached the deck and the breeze hit the phone. "I've got it. Listen for the freakin' splash, sweetheart."

She barely heard a splash before the connection went dead.

AARON SCANNED THE WATER, taking count of the snorkelers, trying to concentrate on anything to take his mind off Charlie.

Bogus marriage or not, how could she think he'd sleep with someone else while they were still married? What kind of lowlife did she take him for?

Eight hours later and blood still pounded through his veins from her call. Grabbing his cigarettes off the table, he lit one and took a long drag. He hadn't wanted that damn phone in the first place. It was like she'd saddled him with a damn umbilical cord.

The woman calling the bungalow was obviously another Thurman stooge hired to cause trouble. For all he cared, Thurman could take a long walk off a short pier, but Charlie?

Screw them both!

He turned back toward the water, listening to the four retired couples laughing. They were totally taken with snorkeling. No glass bottom boats for this crowd. What kind of people would he and Charlie be when they were sixty?

He had to get thoughts like that out of his mind. There was no future. There never had been. She didn't trust him. And she didn't respect him. She might care for him—she definitely cared about him—but he'd never measure up to her standards. There would always be suspicion. He'd always be a low-life, womanizing wharf rat.

Charlie would move back to Boston and marry some guy more in line with her upbringing. Become superwoman. Give one hundred and fifty percent of herself to her family and one hundred and fifty percent to Harrington's. She'd be so committed, she'd lose herself trying to be perfect at both.

He couldn't erase the image of Charlie with another man. He couldn't stomach the thought of some other guy sharing her bed.

He pushed back from the rail and rubbed his arm. God, he was ready to get back in the water. But his arm hurt like hell after the one day he had. The kid from the dive shop that was helping today had things under control, so Aaron decided to check on a couple items at his desk, anything for a distraction.

He opened the bottom drawer and glared at the book he'd bought last week. *Simple Steps to Studying for Your GED.* Simple for who? He slammed the drawer. They should have titled it *The Idiot's Guide to Studying for Your GED.*

Not that a crappy piece of paper would make a difference. He couldn't afford to think like this. He wasn't the man for Charlie. A hell of a lot more than education or the distance between Boston and the Keys separated them.

THE LAST THING AARON WANTED when he dropped the day's receipts off at the resort boutique for Rosa was to run into Charlie. But, as he started through the lobby there was a commotion at the counter. He turned to find two boys with Down syndrome accompanied by their moms. They looked nine or ten and they were shoving each other and grinning from ear to ear.

Rosa touched his arm. "You ought to take them snorkeling."

He smiled at their exuberance and handed her the receipts and checks. "Think their moms would go for that?"

"I bet they'd love the idea."

"Maybe I'll track them down after they get settled in and suggest it."

Rosa stuffed the envelope under her arm. "I need to get these entered and deposited."

The women rounded up the boys and herded them toward the elevator. That was when he caught sight of Charlie. She was standing to the side of the counter, rubbing her forehead, and frowning at the boys. Concern or pity? He backed out of sight.

That's the way Charlie would look at him if she knew.

THE AFTERNOON AARON ARRANGED to take the Down syndrome boys out to the reef, he arrived at the hotel only to be met by Charlie. She was standing with the mothers and talking to the two boys. He glanced suspiciously at her shorts and beach bag.

He nodded at the women and smiled at the kids. "Afternoon. You guys ready to see some cool fish and coral?"

"Yeah. I'm Timmy." The bigger boy beamed. "He's Jon."

Jon clutched his mother's hand and grinned.

Aaron shook hands with Karen, Timmy's mom.

"Hope you don't mind if your wife tags along." Charlie smiled. "I need a break from the office."

Why would she want to go out on the boat with him when Thurman was lurking around? He narrowed his eyes. "I guess we're ready."

She smiled and handed Aaron a box. "Your new cell phone came in."

He took the box and watched her casually stroll toward the boat with Olivia and Karen as if it was the most natural thing in the world that she'd replaced the phone he'd tossed overboard.

Charlotte ignored Aaron's befuddled look and started talking to Karen. She needed this opportunity to be with him. And with her away from the resort, maybe Perry would let his guard down and Security could pick up something on the cameras.

She deposited her beach paraphernalia in the corner and helped him cast off the lines. There wasn't a cloud in the sky today, so hopefully the water would be calm.

Karen and Olivia were exceptional women. They had met through their sons and become fast friends.

The boys' exuberance was contagious. Every activity brought delight to their faces. Both kids could swim, but not well. Aaron made sure they wore flotation devices, making it easy for them to stay on top of the water and use masks to view the undersea world. Charlotte helped Karen with Timmy while Aaron coaxed and worked with the smaller, more timid Jon.

Olivia, Jon's mother, brushed up against Aaron. "You are so patient with him."

Charlotte told herself there was no reason for her twinge of jealousy, but when Aaron beamed back at the woman, Charlotte's heart stopped. "He's a cool kid. Not afraid of anything, are you, buddy?"

Jon grinned at the compliment and stuck his face back in the water.

"It's great that you and Karen take them on trips. They'll love swimming with the dolphins tomorrow." Aaron winked at Jon as he surfaced. "Dolphins are really smart and they even let you touch them." He flashed Olivia another grin. "Don't skip the glass bottom boat in Key West. Kids get to see the reef and fish. And for the adults, they serve champagne while you watch the most awesome sunsets."

Jon bounced. "I have a camera."

Charlotte was so distracted watching Olivia and Aaron that she was caught off guard when a floundering Timmy grabbed her shoulders. Before she could react, she went under with Timmy's weight trapping her beneath the surface. In a panic, she sputtered and clawed to reach air.

Aaron's arms came around her waist and dragged her up until she could gulp in air. He held her against him with one arm and steadied Timmy with the other. She took deep breaths and tried not to frighten Timmy.

"Okay?" Aaron asked.

She nodded, not wanting to call attention to herself. It was hard to speak. "Thanks."

Having had enough swimming for the day, she climbed onboard and unrolled the mat Aaron kept under the bench. She spread the picnic dinner out on the deck, and called the others in.

One would think Olivia might put on a cover-up over her skimpy swimsuit, but no such luck. The boys were eating and passing around pictures of the reef, but both Karen and Olivia had Aaron engaged in conversation. He seemed totally immersed in Karen's story about Timmy's accomplishments. Almost subconsciously the women would touch his hand or giggle to draw his attention their way. And as each spoke, Aaron gave her his undivided attention. Like schoolgirls, they vied for his affection.

Charlotte turned as Jon raced across the deck. "Mom, I saw a fish like this," he squealed.

The women started looking at the pictures the boys brought them and listening to their stories.

Glancing back to Aaron, Charlotte found him staring at her legs. His eyes were molten lava. She blushed, realizing she was sitting on the mat where they'd first made love.

He excused himself, stood, and walked over to stare across the water. She resisted the urge to follow, pleased that she wasn't the only one with memories.

After their picnic Timmy tugged Aaron beside him onto the bench to read one of the brochures. He sat patiently and let the boy sound out the words. At thirteen, Timmy was still struggling with some sounds. Aaron helped him with a couple words, but mostly sat and watched him read as if it was the most interesting thing he could be doing.

She tried to concentrate on the conversation around her, but she couldn't keep her eyes off Aaron and Timmy. She shook off the melancholy and tried not to think about kids, and babies and a family of her own.

When they headed back toward Marathon, Jon clamored to help drive the boat. Olivia seemed surprised that her son took Aaron's hand and left her sitting on the bench visiting with Charlotte and Karen. "He never goes any place without me."

Karen smiled. "I think he's enjoying having a man around to take an interest."

"No wonder why. His own father would rather pretend he

doesn't exist." Olivia frowned, then turned to Charlotte and shrugged. "You two have a wonderful life here."

Charlotte smiled, surprised by the comment. "Yes, we do." She left Timmy and the women scanning for dolphins and went to check on Aaron and Jon.

She stood back, watching the way he related to the child. The boy stood with his legs braced apart, and peering over the steering wheel. The T-shirt Aaron had given him reached to his knees. "I wish you were my dad."

Keeping one hand on the wheel, Aaron helped him guide the boat. "But you already have a dad."

"He's always busy. He never plays with me."

"Well, dads have to work," Aaron said.

Jon chewed his bottom lip and looked as if it was taking every bit of concentration he had to hold the wheel. "I wish he ran a scuba boat and I could help him every day."

"Maybe you could visit him at his job."

"Nope, no kids allowed," Jon said. He looked adorable with the adult-sized blue Brody's cap backward and barely staying on top of his head.

Aaron gripped the wheel as they rode over a wave. "If you were my son and I wasn't spending enough time with you, know what I'd want you to do?"

The cap threatened to topple off as he shook his head. "What?"

"I'd want you to tell me. Sometimes dads get so busy working they forget their kids need them, too."

Jon frowned. "He doesn't have time."

Aaron caught the cap as it fell and placed it back on Jon's head. "Maybe, maybe not. Couldn't hurt to ask."

She exchanged smiles with Aaron and her heart threatened to burst. Every time she thought she had him figured, he surprised her.

She imagined him with his own son, taking him on the

boat, teaching him to swim, snorkel and dive. She did a mental double take. Was that what was going on? She was pushing thirty and she craved a child? Aaron's child.

Olivia took Jon's hand. "Come quick. Look at the dolphins."

Aaron watched him race to the rail, pointing off the starboard side.

Taking a deep breath for courage, Charlotte looked into his eyes. "Aaron, I'm so sorry about the other night."

He shook his head. "Don't worry about it. I overreacted."

"I warned you I'm not good at this romance game."

"We aren't exactly playing on a fair field when it comes to romance." He massaged the back of his neck and tried to smile. "We aren't supposed to win. Remember?"

"Yeah, I know." She fought back the tears and searched for anything to keep from making a fool of herself. "It was nice of you to take the boys out to the cove. You have an admirer in Jon. He stuck under your wing all afternoon."

"Kid needs his dad."

"Yes, he does," she agreed.

He studied her. "Seeing a little of you in Jon?"

"When I was his age, I'd already made up my mind to run a hotel. I didn't understand other kids. I was only interested in shadowing Edward." How did he manage to always draw her out?

He checked the gauges. "I thought little girls dreamed of being princesses. Or maybe an actress like your mom?"

"She didn't have the power Edward had," Charlotte replied, and then stopped. "I've always wanted to be like him."

She glanced at the sunset and decided it paled in comparison to watching Aaron drive. She couldn't tell what he was thinking.

To her amazement, he started talking. "When I was fifteen I

met a team of Navy SEALs. I'm not sure how Whistler got involved, but the plan was to take them out and drop them close enough to board a tanker anchored off Bal Harbor. Man, I thought they were the coolest, toughest guys in the whole world."

"So why didn't you become a SEAL?"

He shrugged, pulling alongside the dock. "Education." He jumped up. "Why don't you help them gather up their stuff? I think I'll hose down the boat then grab a beer at the Gecko."

Not once had Aaron invited her to join him at the Gecko. He obviously didn't want her intruding on his fun, female or otherwise.

He'd just started to open up, but then he'd caught himself. There still seemed like a piece was missing. "See you later."

AARON WATCHED CHARLIE LEAVE. Why had he told her about his dream to be a SEAL? Why not just go ahead and tell her he'd been a hoodlum one step away from getting shot on the streets of Miami? Becoming a SEAL had seemed like his only escape.

Just lay yourself open for ridicule, Brody.

Someone like Charlie, with all her degrees, couldn't begin to understand how even a dream as simple as joining a branch of the military was solar systems out of his reach.

Screw it! There might not be anything he could do about dyslexia, but he was damn tired of hiding from it. He had trouble reading letters and numbers, but he wasn't stupid. Passing the GED wouldn't rescue his marriage, but it would be one step toward feeling better about his lack of education.

Cleaning the boat could wait until morning. He needed a drink.

He walked into the Gecko, waved at Raul, and straddled the only vacant stool at the bar. "Good crowd."

"It's been this way all afternoon. Figured you'd be home with the little wife."

Aaron wrapped his hand around the neck of the frosty amber bottle Raul plunked in front of him. "Don't start."

Raul quirked an eyebrow. "No progress on Thurman?"

"Security has him on camera all day. Rosa has her ear to the resort grapevine. Trust me, he'll screw up soon enough."

"If he does, Rosa will hear about it." Raul drew a beer and took it down the bar to another customer.

A voluptuous brunette squeezed between Aaron and the guy on the next stool. "It's really crowded in here."

He didn't comment.

She leaned around and smiled into his face. "Dance?"

"No."

The girl looked disgruntled with his one word rejection, huffed, and moved on to more willing prey.

The band stunk. What they lacked in rhythm they made up for in noise. You couldn't hear the singer, much less understand the lyrics. Probably a good thing.

God, he was bored with this scene. What was that song? Something about a row of fools and a row of stools. For once, he was ready for Spring Break to end and the village to settle back into some measure of sanity.

He hadn't noticed Raul approach until he spoke. "So why don't you get your ass home to your wife? Make it work."

"Save your advice to the lovelorn for your other patrons." He took a swig of beer.

Raul slammed a bowl of peanuts on the bar. "You're a hardheaded SOB. Never took you for a fool, though."

Aaron swiveled on the stool and took a swig of beer, watching the brunette drag Sal onto the dance floor, wiggling her butt like an excited puppy. "What in hell is keeping that skirt on?" At least there was no sign of the Frenchman tonight.

"A few months ago, you'd have had that lady in bed in thirty minutes flat, but you didn't give her a second look."

Raul glanced at the crowd. "There isn't a lady in this room who can hold a candle to what you've already got, *mi amigo*. And you know it."

Resting his elbows on the bar, he scrubbed both hands across his face. "That's not the point."

"You don't think you're good enough for her?" Raul cleared the empty beer bottle and popped the top on another.

He raised an eyebrow and studied the cold beer. "Can't you hear the sparkling party conversation? Her upper-crust friends are talking about their Ivy League college days and I'm describing what it's like to go Dumpster diving in South Miami."

"If you love the lady, make it work. Your inferiority complex is your problem, not hers." He flashed a knowing grin. "Novel experience to fall in love with one's own wife, yes?"

Aaron tilted his head, but didn't comment.

Raul took a cigarette and held the package out to him. "Smoke?"

He shook his head and shrugged. "Trying to quit."

As he made his way to the bungalow, he chewed on Raul's words. Love? Were they falling in love? Damn close.

Chapter Sixteen

Aaron stuffed a couple changes of clothes into his faded duffel. "I'm booked solid the next sixteen days. It's easier if I sleep on the boat."

Charlotte stepped into his path. "We still need to keep up the pretense until Perry's gone."

"Fine. I'll sleep here two or three nights, but if you're going to make the breakup believable, it's time to start showing signs that things aren't going so well."

Breakup? She swallowed. Intellectually she knew their arrangement was temporary, but not emotionally. "I guess you have a point."

"You have my cell number if you need anything." He opened the back door and made his escape.

Charlotte stared at the door and felt a chunk of her heart go with him. He hadn't stormed off, but his leaving was different tonight. This was the beginning of goodbye.

BY THE THIRD NIGHT AARON didn't come home, Charlotte was climbing the walls. The bungalow was immaculate and quiet, excruciatingly quiet. Everything in its place, everything except the man who belonged in her bed.

The kitchen clock read six-forty-five and she didn't have a single thing on the agenda to fill the evening. She'd talked to the security manager, but he'd told her to go home. They had Perry's every action on tape and would let her know if he did anything suspect.

The old Charlotte would have still been at her desk, but those days were over. There had to be more to life than work, or what was the purpose?

This was ridiculous! Aaron was most likely at The Green Gecko having a good time with his friends. She didn't have to sit here alone. She had as much right as he did to have dinner out.

THE GECKO, AS AARON CALLED IT, vibrated with sound. A wannabe Jennifer Lopez gyrated and crooned on the little platform in the corner. Patrons wandered in and out off the street. The wooden tables were crowded with people drinking and laughing. Even the bar was packed. Charlotte searched every table, but she couldn't spot Aaron. Someone vacated a stool and she quickly took a seat.

The bartender sauntered over, polishing a glass. "What'll it be?"

"Just a bottle of water, please." She continued to scan the faces for her husband. But without the benefit of air-conditioning, the cloud of cigarette smoke hung heavy in the air. A sultry ocean breeze filtered into the open-air bar. A hodge-podge of mounted fish, snapshots of boats and a tattered poster of Ernest Hemingway covered the walls.

The bartender twisted the cap off an Evian and set it in front of her. "He's already come and gone."

"Excuse me?" She looked closer. "I'm sorry. You were at the wedding, right?"

"Raul." He nodded and set the glass he was polishing under the bar.

"Did he say where he was going?"

Raul grabbed the money the guy next to her left and deposited it in the register. "Just said he had things to do. Wasn't too talkative."

"Doesn't care to talk to me, either," she said, studying her tarnished wedding ring as she reached for the frosty water bottle. "Maybe he went back to the *Free Wind*."

"Maybe," Raul said.

She lingered over her water, keeping an eye peeled in case Aaron returned. She must be a glutton for punishment. Even if he did care for her, this relationship was no more than a good time for him. Still she refused to go back to that empty bungalow. Her stomach growled. "What do you have on the menu for dinner?"

"Aaron had a bowl of seafood gumbo." Raul's mouth twitched as if he wanted to grin. "Have you considered the possibility that he might care too much?"

Had she been thinking aloud? "How can someone care too much?" Her logical nature wasn't buying that theory.

The bartender just shrugged.

Sitting here and discussing her relationship with Aaron's friend wasn't the plan. She spotted a tiny table in the corner and picked up her water. "Could you have someone bring a bowl of gumbo over there, please?"

She grabbed the table before two fishermen could and sat. She might not want to be alone, but she didn't want to be grilled, either. She placed her water on the table and hung her purse over the back of the wooden chair.

"You know, men like Aaron aren't good at considering how women feel," Rosa said as she placed a large bowl of gumbo and four cellophane packages of crackers in front of Charlotte. "But he's a good man. You could do worse."

Her cheeks burned. Did everyone on the island know about her relationship with Aaron? "Yeah, he's just great."

Without waiting for an invitation, Rosa sat in the opposite chair and adjusted the neckline on her red satin blouse. "So why don't you look happy?" Her pouty lips and long nails were manicured a deep red to match the blouse. Rosa obviously knew her way around men, and she knew Aaron. How depressing. The only thing Charlotte knew about men was how much she didn't know.

"I am happy." She spooned a bite of gumbo and fought to keep her problems to herself. Couldn't a lady come into a bar to have dinner without half the people butting into her business?

"Honey, between you and Aaron, I don't know who looks more miserable."

Aaron looked miserable? She dropped the spoon and pushed the bowl away without finishing it. "I need a drink."

Rosa snapped her fingers at Raul. "A large pitcher of frozen margaritas and bring out the good tequila."

Charlotte narrowed her eyes at Rosa and picked up her spoon. She'd lost her appetite, but it wasn't a good idea to sit here and drink on an empty stomach.

Raul plunked two salt-rimmed glasses on the table and nudged Rosa. "You behave or a certain scuba guide will be up your ass."

"Bring the pitcher." Rosa gave his butt a quick pat.

Charlotte spooned another bite of gumbo and tried to stay calm. She shouldn't have come here. With all the restaurants and bars on the island, she could have had dinner anywhere. But she tortured herself at the one dive where everyone knew Aaron.

A young waitress plunked a pitcher of green slush on the table and her heavily made-up blue eyes glanced over Charlotte with obvious curiosity.

Rosa waved her away, filled both glasses to the brim, and pushed one toward Charlotte. "This will make you feel better."

She took a drink. The icy liquid both burned and froze her tonsils on its way down. She put a hand to her throat to thaw it out. Raul must have used a half bottle of his expensive tequila.

"Lick the salt," Rosa suggested, taking her own advice.

She touched her tongue to the salt, then chased it with another drink of margarita. The second one went down more smoothly. "So tell me about men, Rosa."

"About men? Or about Aaron?"

It was totally inappropriate to discuss her relationship with an employee. Rosa managed the resort boutique. What if she couldn't keep her mouth shut? "Aaron." She took another gulp of the wonderful slush.

Rosa shook her head. "If you want to know about Aaron, maybe you should ask him."

Fury bubbled to the surface like a long smoldering volcano. Charlotte grabbed her glass, licked the rim, and swallowed half the contents. "What makes you think he'd talk to me? He won't even stay at the bungalow." Well, that sounded like a whiny wife.

"*Mejia.*" Rosa took a long drink of her own margarita. "If you want Aaron, you've got to let him know. Tell him how you feel."

True panic set in. Tell him how she felt, knowing he didn't return her love? No way.

"How do you feel about your husband, *mejia?*" Rosa's soft voice coaxed.

Feelings trembled through Charlotte in total chaos. Fury, confusion, love. "I love him, Rosa." She swallowed a frozen lump blocking her throat and it wasn't slushy margarita.

"Okay? So, what's wrong with that?" Rosa narrowed her eyes. "He's your husband."

Charlotte sniffed and rubbed one hand under her eyes. "It's all an act. We're not really married. I mean we are, but it isn't real." She jabbed her hands through her hair. "We both had our own reasons to pretend."

Rosa filled both glasses. "But you're not pretending any longer?"

"I messed up and fell in love." Charlotte drank and put her glass down. The room spun, but she ignored it. "Every day I can't wait to get home and see him."

"Does he know you're in love with him?"

Charlotte shook her head. "I can't tell him."

Rosa swirled her drink in the glass and studied it as it sloshed dangerously close to the rim. "Why not? He might surprise you."

She took a sip for courage. "He's made his feelings clear. He has no desire to have a family and spend the rest of his life connected to me. Aaron can have—has had—his pick of women." She swallowed another sip. The room was definitely spinning. "Isn't this stupid? I'm in love with my husband and can't tell him."

Rosa ran one red-tipped finger around the rim of her empty glass until it sang. "Don't try to make love logical. I'm divorced three times and still half in love with two of them."

Charlotte followed the direction of Rosa's gaze, not sure she'd heard her correctly. "Raul?"

"Of course. Such a sexy hunk. We just get along better when we aren't married."

Charlotte slugged down the rest of her drink. "Wow!"

Rosa refilled their glasses. "We're quite a pair, aren't we?" She swirled the green slush. "What do I do?"

Rosa clicked her glass against Charlotte's. "We're going to rock Aaron's world. Leave it to me."

Charlotte frowned at the giant marlin mounted on the back wall. Was it swimming toward her? "You don't understand. I paid Aaron to marry me. It's a business arrangement."

"That doesn't mean he can't fall in love."

"I'll soon be living in Boston and helping my grandfather run the business."

"Is that what you really want?"

Charlotte shrugged. "I...I don't know."

"Do you want to make your marriage work?"

She downed the rest of her drink. "Oh, God, yes."

Rosa leaned back and drained her own glass. "Then we have work to do."

WHEN AARON ARRIVED AT THE Gecko, he found Charlie and Rosa huddled together at a small table in the back whispering and giggling like schoolgirls. An empty pitcher sat between them and two large margarita glasses were stacked one on top of the other.

When Raul called and told him he needed to come pick up his drunken wife, he hadn't believed him. Luckily, he knew Charlie kept the spare key to her Volvo in the nightstand.

Rosa waved at him, stood, and grabbed the pitcher. "Hey, good-lookin'. How about jogging over to the bar and refilling this for two sexy ladies?"

He caught the pitcher she tossed in his direction. "Looks to me like these two sexy ladies have had enough for one night." Charlie had both elbows propped on the table and was literally holding her head up. She was barely conscious.

Rosa strolled around him as if she were checking out a side of beef. He looked to make sure his fly was zipped.

She came to a stop in front of him and winked. "If you'll spring for another pitcher, you can join our party."

What was going on here? Charlie and Rosa were drunk as sailors and it wasn't even midnight. He slipped his arm around Charlie and pulled her to her feet. "I think it's time my wife went home."

Charlie tried to stand, but she was as limp as a rag doll. It had been a long time since he'd been that drunk, but he remembered the feeling distinctly. He scooped her into his arms and gave Rosa a scowl. "You can catch the tab on this little party."

Charlie focused her glassy stare on him and twirled the front of his hair with her finger. "That little curl gives you a sexy, rakish look," she slurred.

"Rakish, huh?" She looked messy and adorable.

Rosa caught his arm. "Charlotte's a wunnerful woman."

What had triggered that? "Yes, she is."

"You hurt my boss and you'll have me to reckon with, buster." She wagged a finger in his face.

It was all he could do not to laugh. "I'm shaking in my sneakers."

She nodded as if that settled everything, and then mumbled, "You should. Ms. Harrington wants a hunk, then Ms. Harrington should have a hunk."

He headed toward the door for a second time. Charlie blew a silky tendril of hair out of her eyes. "Where're you taking me?"

"Home."

Rosa gave Charlie the thumbs-up.

Charlie tried to wink, but both eyes closed. "Cool."

Raul said they'd been together all evening. Aaron narrowed his eyes at Rosa and lugged his wife toward the Volvo, barely resisting the urge to toss her over his shoulder like a he-man with his wench. He grinned at how Charlotte Harrington Brody would take to that.

She was deadweight when he tried to pull her out of the car at the bungalow. He picked her up again and carried her into the house. He flipped on the light, steadied her in a sitting position on the bed, and grabbed a nightshirt out of the drawer. By the time he finally maneuvered her into bed and smoothed the sheet up, she was almost asleep.

"Kiss." She puckered her pretty lips. "Knight in shining armor always kisses princess."

He wasn't sure, but it seemed like she was mixing up her fairy tales. He smoothed the hair back from her face and brushed her lips with his. "Good night, princess."

He turned out the light and shook his head. Charlie and Rosa? Charlie might be a rookie in the romance game, but Rosa was a seasoned general. He was in deep shit with her switching her allegiance to Charlie's team.

Chapter Seventeen

Aaron hesitated outside the bungalow door. He rolled his shoulders to scratch the itch from his black shirt. He'd been suspicious since Charlie had insisted he let her make him dinner as repayment for looking after her the night before.

Something didn't feel right. There was more to the itch than a starched shirt.

He opened the door and the succulent aroma of prime rib made his mouth water. Candles and flickering firelight cast shadows across a white linen cloth spread on the floor and covered with china and sparkling crystal.

Before he could digest that, Charlie strolled out of the kitchen. At least he thought it was her. She flipped a mass of curls over her shoulder. Bare feet peeped from beneath a flowing tropical skirt and the loose white halter was like nothing he'd ever seen. One shoulder was strapless and the shadow of her dark nipples teased him through the thin cotton.

He licked his lips as a sharp ache hit his gut. He swallowed and forced his stare to move upward to her face.

Rosa was behind this. Charlie shifted her shoulders and pink glossy lips curved up in an enticing smile. "Hi."

"Char—" He cleared his throat. "Charlie?"

Her smile faltered a second and she leaned forward to

place a silver ice bucket on the corner of the tablecloth. Her top fell away and he gulped at the glimpse of bare breast.

"Hope you don't mind eating here?" She straightened and smoothed her skirt down her flat stomach. Her hands framed the V of her pubic area before sliding slowly down her thighs.

Charlie wouldn't do that on purpose. Would she?

"—relaxing end to a long day." He had no idea what she'd been saying. A roar that had nothing to do with the sound of the surf through the open windows echoed in his ears. He should get out of here while he had a chance. Every night he spent with Charlie made leaving more difficult. Damn Rosa.

Charlie's gaze raked over him. "Get comfortable."

"Okay." He kicked his docksiders in the corner, but he felt anything but comfortable. He couldn't stop staring at the sexy sway of her hips as she glided in and out of the kitchen, arranging a feast on the tablecloth in front of the fire.

She came out balancing two plates and flashed him a sexy little grin. "Don't just stand there. Open the wine." A mysterious, almost smile played at the corners of her mouth. Oh, God. Why hadn't he made a run for the door when he had the chance? This evening was going to be a drill in self-control. How was he supposed to keep his distance when she'd turned into a sexy gypsy seductress?

"Aaron, are you all right?"

Snapping out of his thoughts, he lowered himself to the floor and grabbed the corkscrew. "I figured we'd go out." He sounded like a tongue-tied kid.

Charlie added a basket of bread and sat beside him, bending one knee under her and not bothering to pull her flowing skirt below midthigh where it had landed. "You're always cooking for me. Thought you might enjoy a change."

Rod Stewart played at a muted volume in the background about tonight being the night. Not Charlie's typical playlist. He handed her a glass of wine and noticed that her nails were painted bright pink. Who was this woman? "Like your hair."

Twisting a curl between two fingers, she looked sheepish. "You do? I wasn't sure how it would turn out, but the stylist insisted that I'd feel like a new woman."

New woman? She was a sizzling temptress. He resisted the urge to ask if Rosa had chosen the outfit. "It's nice." Nice? Geesh, what was he, fifteen? Her hair was everything but nice. Sexy, seductive, untamed, wicked—

She picked up her fork and stabbed a bite of chilled shrimp cocktail. "Thanks," she said as she methodically coated the pink morsel in sauce. She gazed into his eyes as she slowly brought it to her lips, closed her eyes and moaned.

Breathe, Brody. It was just shrimp. He adjusted his position and focused on his own salad. Maybe a drink of wine? Or the whole bottle.

Aaron tried to ignore her, but never in his life had he seen a woman make a simple meal seem so erotic. He topped off his wine, but Charlie had barely taken a sip of hers.

She used each morsel to torture him. The steak was tender and juice dribbled on her lips. But instead of using a napkin, she snaked her tongue out to swipe it away. Minutes passed in a daze as he pictured her adept tongue licking his chin and working her way down every inch of his body. Dammit! Charlie brought her glass to her lips and hesitated ever so slowly before taking a dainty sip. Even that turned him on.

He wiped his mouth and leaned back on his elbows, trying to look anywhere but at Charlie's butt as she sashayed to the kitchen. She returned with crème brûlée and knelt at his side, her breasts brushing his arm. Heat rocketed through him kicking his overloaded libido into overdrive.

She stared into his eyes, scooped a small bite and held it to his lips. "See what you think. Pierre is a master."

Against his better judgment, he allowed her to spoon-feed him. Before he could swallow, she leaned forward and licked the corner of his mouth.

He turned to capture her lips, but she moved away. The bungalow had been chilly when he arrived, but the temperature just shot off the top of the thermostat.

Two could play at this game. He scooped a bite onto his finger. "Your turn." He deliberately smeared a little on her top lip then covered her mouth in a slow penetrating kiss.

She sighed into his mouth and ran her palms over his chest. He undid the strap and slid her blouse off her shoulder, but she pushed him away.

Shaking her head, her hair swirled around her shoulders. She swiped her finger in the dessert dish and placed a dab of creamy pudding behind his ear, trailing her finger down his throat, before moving in for the kill, licking and suckling her way around his neck and down his chest. His body burned.

Aaron sunk two fingers in the cream and pushed her back onto the carpet. All restraint gone, he eased her top lower and smeared crème brûlée over both breasts, circling the nipples. Stifling a low moan, he licked every last drop clean.

She unbuttoned his shirt and ran her hands over his chest, pinching his nipples. He gave up all attempts at control as her fingers unzipped his slacks and shoved them down. He hadn't noticed her dip her hand in the velvety dessert until it wrapped around him.

Cupping her head between his hands, he adjusted his hips to give her better access. He'd had good sex, incredible one-night stands and a couple of tight relationships, but nothing came close to Charlie.

He didn't know what to make of her. He was totally and completely consumed by his wife.

CHARLOTTE WAS STILL DISTRACTED by Aaron and the night before when Perry dropped into the chair in front of her desk. "I just talked to tech support. Someone changed the code."

"I wonder who could have done that?" she asked, snapping back into work mode. She knew as well as Perry did that he had tampered with the code that programmed the card keys just so he could be the hero, again.

He ignored her sarcasm. "We need to talk."

"About what?"

He rubbed one hand across his mouth and sighed. "I've got a confession."

"Really?" Now she was definitely suspicious.

"I've been worried about you." He paused for effect. The man should be an actor. "I hired a P.I. to keep an eye on Aaron."

"You what?"

"Before you get your dander up, hear me out. I know you love him, but sometimes love's blind. I've made no secret of the fact that I don't trust him."

She jumped to her feet. "You have no right to interfere in my private life."

"Calm down and listen. Your husband is running cocaine on the *Free Wind*."

"What?"

"We suspect they're using The Green Gecko as a meeting place. Lots of commotion there and nobody pays much attention to anybody else's business," Perry pointed out. "One of the guys he drinks with is a known runner. It looks like a small operation, but enough volume to put him away."

She swallowed a lump in her throat. "That's outrageous. Aaron doesn't run drugs."

"Sal Hernandez has a record as long as your arm and the cops have him in their scope. My guy saw him with Aaron." He took a deep breath. "Why do you think he got so bent out of shape when he found me on the boat that night? He knew I was on to him and looking for evidence."

"I don't believe you."

"Charlotte, you've been protected from opportunists like Aaron. His type is smooth and cunning. He'll do whatever it takes to convince you he has your best interest at heart, right up until the moment you realize he's gone and so is your money."

"Sounds like someone else I remember."

His eyes narrowed. "Pull your head out of the sand. The guy's bad news. So far, I've been able to keep the cops off Aaron's trail, but eventually they're going to catch on. If you don't care about yourself, think about the resort. Headline— 'Marathon Key, Harrington Resort Manager's Husband Busted for Drugs.' Can you imagine what that'll do for business?"

She leaned her head against the wall. Perry was only attempting to discredit Aaron, but her business couldn't afford the risk. The rumor alone could hurt not only the Marathon resort, but the entire Harrington chain. Edward would yank her out of here so fast, he wouldn't give her time to pack. And she could forget another manager position. There wasn't a decent resort in the world that would touch her.

Aaron did spend a lot of evenings at The Green Gecko and nights on the *Free Wind*. She had to know for sure.

AARON SAT AT THE POLISHED BAR at Harrington's and nursed a Cognac. It was already past seven and according to Rosa, Thurman stopped by every evening for a nightcap.

"Mind if I join you?" Perry asked, sitting on the stool next to him and motioning the bartender to bring him the same thing Aaron was drinking.

Right on time. "Yeah, I do," he replied, looking over Thurman's navy pin-striped suit. Didn't want the guy to know he was waiting on him.

Perry flashed a toothy smile and pretended he was teasing.

"Don't you think it's time we called a truce? We both care about Charlotte."

"Do we?" Aaron asked, swirling the amber liquid around the snifter. "I thought I cared about her and you were trying to take over her hotel."

The muscles in Perry's jaw twitched. "You want me to believe you're in love with her? I've been in your shoes, remember? Charlotte Harrington is about as sexy as a dead fish."

Aaron flexed his fingers, warning himself not to play into Thurman's hands. "Brody, Charlotte Brody." He nodded toward the piano player in the corner of the room. "Charlie's like that beautiful piano over there." He kicked back and took a slow drink of Cognac. "No matter how perfectly tuned, still depends on who sits down at the keyboard."

"Don't try and play me, Brody. I know she paid you a hundred grand to marry her and save her from Harrington's plan."

"Damn, Percy." Aaron furrowed his brow. "How bad a lay do you have to be that a woman would pay that kind of money to avoid marrying you?"

Perry shoved back from the bar. "You won't be so smug when I expose you for the money-hungry gigolo you are."

He watched Thurman storm out. Wounded male ego was a bitch. The idiot never even took a drink of the expensive liquor.

The bartender raised one eyebrow and cleared away the glass. "I'll put this on his tab."

He had to protect Charlie from guys like Thurman. He wondered if it ever occurred to anyone, including her, that she needed protecting. She acted so together, as if she had her life completely under control.

If it was the last thing he did for her, Aaron was going to bring Thurman down. The SOB was dangerous.

By the time Charlie finally joined him, Aaron had made up his mind not to mention Perry's threat. The way he figured it, if Perry was putting his energy into destroying him, maybe that would give her some breathing room.

When she entered the bar, she'd twisted her hair up and clipped it to the back of her head. Before she'd left the bungalow this morning she'd tied it back in a loose ponytail. Her tight expression worried him. This whole Perry thing was taking more of a toll on her than she'd admit.

Aaron wrapped an arm around her shoulder and bent to give her a kiss. She didn't turn away, but she didn't return the gesture, either.

"Rough day?" He picked up his drink and followed her to one of the tables.

He set his glass down and held out her chair. She placed her purse in one of the empty chairs and glanced at the waiter. "A glass of Chardonnay, please." She turned to answer Aaron's question, but she didn't look him in the eye. "It was long. I need to eat and then get some sleep."

The meal progressed in silence. She looked like it took all her energy just to bring her fork to her mouth. What had changed? Something was bothering her, but she wasn't talking.

Charlotte wasn't sure how she'd gotten through dinner. After his reaction about the phone calls, she couldn't give Aaron any hint that she doubted him. He'd never forgive her.

As soon as they arrived at the bungalow, Aaron undressed and crawled into bed. He looked as exhausted as she felt, but for her, sleep didn't come. She took a hot bath and two aspirin, but neither worked. The more tired she was, the harder time she had sleeping. Add the seeds of doubt that Perry had planted and sleep was elusive. She forced herself to stay in bed until the alarm went off before heading to the office. Aaron was still asleep when she let herself out the door.

How could she know for sure? Calling the cops was out of

the question. They'd ask too many questions about why she was asking questions. She didn't want to focus any unnecessary attention on Aaron. So, if she couldn't ask Aaron directly and she couldn't consult the police, what other options were available?

Rosa? She did keep Aaron's books. And she was right here in the resort. Problem was that Rosa was Aaron's friend long before she was Charlotte's.

She had to give it a shot.

Chapter Eighteen

Aaron had hardly set foot inside the Gecko when Rosa stomped up to him, her dark eyes flashing sparks. "You need to tell me what's going on."

"What're you talking about?" He'd never seen her look so ticked off at anyone except Raul.

She tapped her high heel and glared at him as if he should be able to read her mind. "Why is your wife asking me all these questions? I no more than get back from lunch than here she comes."

His suspicion meter shot off the chart. "What kind of questions?"

"Do I know Sal Hernandez? Do you talk to anyone suspicious? Why would she ask something like that?"

"I have no idea. What else?"

"Were your books on the level? Had I noticed anything out of line? Said she was curious about your buddies, but then she clammed up." Rosa grabbed a drink order off the bar, delivered it to the two guys at the corner table, then tossed the tray back on the bar.

She didn't miss a beat in her tirade. "She told me to forget the conversation and not to tell you! Right? Like who does she think she is? I mean, why would I not tell you?"

Something was up and Thurman was behind it. If he'd managed to plant more suspicions in Charlie's head, then why didn't she come to him? Same reason she didn't come to him about the phone calls. The woman didn't trust him. Never had. Never would. "Anything else?"

"That's pretty much it, but if she does it again and I lose my temper, and probably my job, you better be prepared to support me."

"If Raul couldn't afford you, what makes you think I can?" he teased, or tried to.

She didn't smile. Rosa was the one person he trusted. She knew about his problem and didn't look down on him. "I've been thinking about buying a laptop so we could put my books on it. I don't want anything in that resort she can go through."

"You have nothing to hide, Aaron."

"You and Raul know that. But Charlie doesn't." Aaron gave her a quick hug. "I don't want Charlie to know about the computer for a while. And I need you to watch that temper, stay at the resort, and keep your ear to the ground. See if you can find out what female Thurman paid to make those calls to Charlie."

"Oh! I almost forgot." Rosa stepped back and her eyes sparkled. "That flighty secretary of hers likes to gloat. Today she came down to the break room to get a soda and I heard her mouthing off to Grace that Miss High and Mighty was on her way out. Perry Thurman would be running things soon and then she'd be set. Zelda said Perry was going to put her up in her own place and she wouldn't have to be taking orders from that bitch anymore."

"Zelda is sleeping with Thurman?"

"Morning, noon and night."

Aaron couldn't say he was shocked, but he hadn't figured that angle. "If he's using her to snoop into Charlie's personal affairs, then he could find out all sorts of things to sabotage her, or me for that matter."

Rosa's haughty nose turned up. "Well, I don't want him to hurt you, but after the little episode with your wife this afternoon, I'm not feeling too sympathetic toward her."

"Give her a break. She just doesn't know how to get close to people."

"You deserve someone who will at least trust you. Somebody with a heart."

He patted her shoulder. "You knew she had a heart even before I did. She just sucks at people skills."

"Maybe." She nudged her way between him and the guy standing at the bar next to him. "So what's Perry Thurman's problem?"

He took a swig of beer. "Terminal asshole. Why?"

She flopped down on the next stool. "I haven't told you about the rest of my sucky day. Thurman comes waltzing into the boutique shortly after Charlotte left and starts asking even more questions than your wife. Said he'd seen the two of us together and practically accused us of being lovers. Wanted to know if you were as good as your reputation, one-hundred-thousand-dollars good."

Raul set a glass of wine in front of her and leaned on the bar, eager to hear the rest of the story.

"So, what did you tell him?" Aaron asked.

"I suggested he ask his boss about her husband's skills between the sheets, if that was his bent, but I figured he was wasting his time. Didn't think he was your type."

Raul chortled.

"Crap. I'm just generating all sorts of interest today. Raul, anybody come around grilling you?"

Raul refilled a bowl of peanuts. "Nope, but I doubt I can think as fast as Rosa."

"Put the lady's wine on my tab."

Rosa shook her head. "The lady wants dinner."

Raul leaned toward Aaron and whispered loud enough for Rosa to hear. "She eats when she's angry."

"Dinner it is," Aaron agreed. "'Cause I guaran-damn-tee you that Perry Thurman can make a person angrier than anybody I've ever met."

They found an empty table and the waiter had just set their plates in front of them when Aaron's cell phone rang. He fished it out of his pocket and punched the button.

"Can you come home?"

He closed his eyes. Last night, she'd hardly spoken to him. "What's wrong?" he asked, pushing away from the table.

"I just need to talk to you."

He wasn't sure he was up to another disgruntled female tonight. Especially one who didn't trust him enough to be honest about whatever it was she was snooping around about.

AARON WALKED INTO THE BUNGALOW and Charlie descended on him like a hurricane of swirling words. "Perry's having an affair with Zelda. Zelda! Can you believe that? Security filmed her going into Perry's room upstairs, five minutes after he went in. Then a half hour later, she comes waltzing out, her hair looking like a rat had slept in it."

"One had." Aaron's gaze followed her as she paced back and forth. Something told him this whole come-home-and-talk scene had more to it than Thurman's new bed partner. It'd be nice if Charlie would level with him about whatever lies Thurman was feeding her. "Rosa told me this afternoon. I figure Perry's using Zelda to stay on top of what you're up to and getting a little action as a fringe benefit. Do you think she's the one who was making those calls?"

"I'd recognize her voice, but she could have a friend or someone do it." Charlie tapped her foot. "Guess what else.

When more reservations turned up cancelled today I called tech support. They've all been changed under Maria's sign-in, but here's the kicker. One workstation, Zelda's. Maria's been with the resort for years. I trust her. So I figure Perry somehow got her password and gave it to Zelda. I had Maria change her password. But, first thing tomorrow morning, Zelda's history."

Aaron shook his head. "Not so fast. She may come in handy to help us nail Thurman."

"He had the supplier put the shipment of toilet paper in the basement instead of the storeroom. The cleaning staff ran completely out today and when I called the supplier they assured me they delivered twenty-five cases yesterday." She closed her eyes and took a deep breath. "I happened to go down to the basement to check on the wine and there was all this toilet paper."

A creative move, even for Thurman. "That's pretty crappy."

Her mouth dropped open and she looked as if she might reply, but she evidently didn't find the humor in his pun. "What else is he up to?" she asked, more to herself than him.

Somebody pounded on the front door. Charlie walked over to the door and jerked it open. "Can I help you?"

"Is Brody here? Tell him it's Sal and I have to talk to him. Now."

Aaron caught the suspicion in Charlie's expression as she turned from the door. He eased by her, joined Sal on the front porch, and closed the door. "What are you doing here?"

"I just left the police station. *Alguien dijo ellos que corría las drogas.* Any idea who might have told them something like that?"

"Drugs? How the hell should I know?"

Sal was angrier than both women combined. "They think I'm using your boat to transport them!"

Aaron led him away from the door so hopefully Charlie couldn't overhear. "Why would they think that?"

"I figure you're into something and trying to shift the blame to me." Sal jerked his arm out of Aaron's grasp.

Aaron jabbed both hands through his hair. "So that's what Thurman's spreading."

Sal's fist clenched and unclenched. "What's Thurman got to do with it? He and I get along."

"He's out to destroy me and you're a pawn, my friend."

"You're saying Thurman set the cops on me?"

Aaron leaned back against a palm tree and fought to keep his temper under wrap. "He's setting me up and using you to do it. I better get back to the boat before he plants something on it. Keep your eyes open. I wouldn't be surprised if he's taking pictures of us right now."

"I don't want more trouble with the law. I got a family."

"Your best bet is to stay away from me. Don't give Thurman any ammunition."

Sal headed down the sidewalk mumbling in Spanish about dismembering certain body parts of Thurman's and fish food.

Aaron opened the door of the bungalow and Charlie stepped back. She was as white as the alabaster walls and her mouth set in a grim line. He returned her glare. At this point he had to stay out of jail. If she chose to believe Thurman's lies, why waste time defending himself?

He shoved past her, stuffed what clothes he could find into his duffel, retrieved his razor and toothbrush from the bathroom, and looked around for anything else.

"So you're running away?" Charlie glared as he came back into the living room.

"I'm protecting myself and my business. I'll be on the boat." He didn't wait for her to respond. Who else was he going to have to fight tonight? Apparently, the whole freakin' island thought he was up to something illegal.

PERRY MET CHARLOTTE IN FRONT of Zelda's desk when she arrived the next morning and dogged her into the office. "Where have you been? The bride in 315 called the cops on her new husband last night and we had three cruisers out front for two hours. I couldn't even get them to turn off the flashing lights. You didn't answer your phone."

"I was asleep." She'd given in and taken a sleeping pill after Aaron left. When Sal Hernandez had come to the door, she'd heard two words that sent chills down her spine: *drugs* and *police*.

"This place is going down the tubes, but I'm so happy that Charlotte got her beauty rest," Perry said sarcastically as he slammed her office door on his way out.

She winced. She wasn't awake enough to deal with Perry.

She asked Zelda to bring her coffee. Sleeping pills always made her groggy the next day.

As Zelda brought in the coffee, Charlotte's cell rang. What else could go wrong today?

The security guy sounded pleased. "Thurman is talking to two Hispanic males. We picked up part of the conversation over the chaos in the lobby. Something about tonight and Thurman handed the lanky one a brown envelope."

She waited until Zelda left the office before answering. "Keep an eye on them and call me back on my cell as soon as they start to leave. Don't use the hotel line." The last thing they needed was for Zelda to get wind of what was going on and tip Perry off.

She hung up and dialed Aaron. "Aaron, Perry is talking to two Hispanic males in the lobby."

"I'm on the way."

As soon as Security said the men were leaving, she quickly dialed Aaron and gave him their description and whereabouts.

AARON WAITED UNTIL THE TWO guys walked off the resort grounds, then came up behind them and put an arm on each of their shoulders. "Got a second?"

The skinny guy pulled away, but Aaron held on to the hefty one. "Look, guys. I know you were the two on the *Free Wind* that night."

"We don't know nothin' about the *Free Wind*." The skinny one seemed to be the mouthpiece for the duo.

"If you'd rather talk to the cops than me, that's cool, too."

That woke up the big guy. "We got no reason to talk to no cops. You got no proof."

Aaron grinned. "Harrington's has top-of-the-line surveillance cameras. Amazing what those things can pick up. Crystal clear sound. They know which pocket you put the envelope in that Thurman gave you. Hell, they can zoom in and read the insignia on that ring."

The guys exchanged glances. The skinny one twisted the ring and lost some of his macho. "So what do you want from us?"

"Tell me what Thurman is paying you to do tonight."

"We can't do that," the big guy said.

"Here's the deal, guys. I don't really give a shit about you two, but Thurman's going down. So you have two choices. I hand you over to the police and you take your chances whether you go down with him. Or you can help me out."

AARON NEVER THOUGHT HE'D WALK into a police station of his own free will, but by the time he left, he felt slightly more confident. At least Officer Perez had listened to his story and not thrown him out on his ear, or locked him up.

Next stop was the lawyer's office to file the divorce papers, then the bank. He had to do right by Charlie. Once Thurman was out of the picture, the quicker and cleaner he and Charlie could end this, the less painful it would be.

He called Charlie's cell and told her to have Zelda make dinner reservations on one of the other islands.

"Tell her you're meeting me there, then get in your car and go. I need Thurman to think the boat's deserted."

"But you're going to be waiting for him?" She sounded panicked. "Aaron, don't do anything stupid."

"Thurman's not calling the shots this time." He hung up before she could argue.

CHARLOTTE DID WHAT AARON ASKED and then drove to the restaurant. He wasn't going to show, but she still had to stay away from the bungalow or Perry would see her car. She might as well have dinner.

Thoughts of Aaron in danger, lying hurt…or worse filled her mind. Minutes ticked by like hours. As tempted as she was to call, she held off. Just her luck the phone would ring right in the middle of whatever he was up to and tip Perry off.

She lingered over dinner and didn't return to the bungalow until after ten. No sign of Aaron. No message on her machine. Nothing to give her any hint what was going on or even that he wasn't at the bottom of the ocean. Didn't the man realize she was a nervous wreck?

Maybe the romance novel would at least take her mind off Aaron. Two hours later, she swiped at tears and closed the book, trying not to think about her own marriage. She hated happy endings. They were totally asinine. Nothing to do with reality.

THE NEXT MORNING, SHE STILL hadn't heard from Aaron. But Edward met her at her office door, ushered her inside, and locked the door behind them. She hadn't even realized her grandfather was in town.

"You'd better sit down."

Charlotte didn't like his stance. Whatever he wanted to say was not good news.

Edward dropped a nondescript report on her desk. "I had Brody checked out." He held up one hand. "Before you jump all over me, keep in mind, I did it to protect you and the business."

The report taunted her.

He slid it closer. "Read it. Don't you want to know the man you married?"

She couldn't bring herself to touch it. If Aaron hadn't told her himself, then she had no business knowing. "I know everything I need to about him."

Edward jerked the report off her desk. "Is this the man you want to spend the rest of your life with? Have children with?" He took his glasses from his breast pocket and shoved them onto his nose. "To begin with, there isn't a father's name on Aaron Brody's birth certificate. Brody is his mother's name. He didn't graduate from high school."

"I know all that."

"Did you also know he's a thief? Did time in reform school. Juvenile drinking. Violent temper. Two cases of assault. Nearly killed another kid when he was fifteen."

Charlotte shook her head. She didn't want to hear any more.

"His mother was a whore. Never married. Died of syphilis. He didn't even have the decency to give her a civilized burial. Scattered her ashes out to sea."

She cringed. "Aaron was sixteen years old when his mother died."

"Did he tell you the navy turned him down because he's illiterate? The reform school diagnosed him with dyslexia."

Dyslexia? She closed her mouth and let that sink in. Dyslexia. One hand came up to rub her eyes. Could that be the secret he was so determined to hide? That would explain him making an excuse and having her read the newspaper article to him that day on the boat. And he'd told her lawyer to give him the *Reader's Digest* version of the prenuptial agreement. Watching Timmy read on the boat…

AARON DOCKED THE *FREE WIND* and found Rosa waiting on the wharf. If she smiled any wider, her makeup was going to crack. She boarded, laid something on his desk, and then helped the passengers disembark. When they were finally alone, she rushed to hand him the envelope. "We've got it."

"What?"

"I happened to be in Grace's office finishing up my paper-work when she was closing out this month's books. She couldn't get them to balance. So, she's looking through entries one by one and she comes across some things that don't add up. She thinks Thurman's embezzling."

He grabbed her around the waist and spun her around. "Oh, darlin'! You made my day." He sat her back on the deck and looked her in the eye. "How sure is she?"

"Grace is still looking, but she's convinced that since Mr. Harrington asked him to keep an eye on the books, Thurman's been skimming. She and I had that slick pegged from day one."

Aaron fished a hundred dollars out of his pocket and handed it to her. "Buy yourself something." He handed her another fifty. "Take Grace to lunch."

He locked the boat down and headed to the bungalow. He sensed something was wrong the minute he walked through the back door. It was too quiet. Charlie should be home by now. He pitched the envelope Rosa had given him on the kitchen table and another paper caught his attention.

He slid the sheet across the table so he could read what it said. What was this?

He blinked at the words. *Arrested for theft. Mother, Jenny Marie Brody, prostitute.* The words blurred. How did they know what she died of?

Charlie had him investigated!

He shoved his hair out of his eyes, his defenses accelerating into full throttle. It was like passing a bloody car crash. You shouldn't stare, but morbid curiosity wouldn't let you look away.

Put a kid in the hospital at age fifteen. Yeah, well the jerk shouldn't have called his mother a whore.

Assault with intent to kill Anthony Morales. Aaron rubbed the back of his neck. They even knew about that last slime bag his mother lived with.

Spent time in reform school.

He flinched when he saw Charlie standing in the doorway. "So, did you find out everything you wanted to know?"

"Edward did this, not me." Her brown eyes pooled with tears. "Aaron, none of this matters. It's all in the past."

His temples pounded and he curled his fingers into a fist and tried to keep from punching a hole in the wall. This wasn't any of Charlie's business and it sure as hell wasn't Harrington's. They could believe whatever they wanted about him, but his mom didn't deserve this. "My mother was a kid herself struggling to survive and raise a kid." The blood pumped through his veins so hard he could feel every beat of his heart. "She was a hotel maid. Her greatest ambition was to be a waitress for God's sake, because they earned tips. Sometimes she got involved with men, none of them good. She was younger than I am now when she died."

Tears trickled down Charlie's cheek as she reached out to touch him. He jerked away. "One of the last guys she moved in with got his jollies knocking her around. Made him feel macho. She was sick, but we didn't know what was wrong because we didn't have money for doctors. One night she was cooking dinner and did something that pissed him off. He grabbed her hair and shoved her against the stove. I lost it. Second offense. They shipped me off to reform school for three months and a crash course in anger management." He focused on his fists and tried to unclench them.

Charlotte took a step toward him.

Too many memories surfacing at once. He choked down the emotion threatening to drown him. "She didn't show up to visit me. I couldn't find her after I got out. Someone else was living in the apartment. I tracked her to a shelter. She was in bad shape. They'd gotten her a doctor." He rubbed his eyes with the palms of his hands. "Screw my probation. Screw school. I started working full-time on Whistler's boat, found a two-room apartment, and watched my mom wither away." He glared at Charlie. "Want to hear more?"

She reached her hand out. "No. Aaron, stop."

She'd started this with that damn report so she could damn well listen. "I barely made enough to pay the rent, so I stole whatever she needed. Food. Medicine. I didn't talk to anybody. Didn't even tell Whistler until right at the end when I couldn't leave her. He helped pay to have her cremated and we scattered her ashes at sea."

"Sit down." Charlie put her hands on his shoulders and guided him into a chair. "I had no idea." She rested one hand against his cheek and sat across from him. He watched as her eyes narrowed. "Why didn't you tell me you were dyslexic?"

He shoved her hand away and bolted up. "Dammit, is there anything you don't know? You're so quick to judge."

"No, Aaron. It's not like that. I'm so sorry, so very sorry for what you've been through."

"I don't want your pity, Charlotte." Without giving her time to stop him, he slammed out the door. He was halfway to the boat before he remembered he hadn't told her about Thurman embezzling.

Chapter Nineteen

Charlotte's heart was breaking for Aaron. She hated herself for forcing all those painful memories to the surface. What kind of person was she? She was worse than Edward. Her grandfather might have instigated the investigation, but she'd allowed Aaron to see it. Nothing in that report mattered.

She wanted to go to Aaron and hold him, but he'd made his feelings clear last night. He didn't want her.

She sat at her desk, going through the motions of work. Edward was getting the resort ready to put on the market, but she no longer cared. All she could think about was the devastation on Aaron's face.

The intercom buzzed. Charlie stared at it a minute before answering. "Yes, Zelda."

"There's a courier here."

Charlotte stood and opened the door.

The courier asked her name, made her sign a receipt, and handed her a registered envelope.

She closed the door and sat back down at her desk. The letter was from the lawyer who had drawn up the prenuptial. She already knew what was inside. She just wasn't sure she could stand seeing the words in black and white.

Taking a deep breath, she slid her finger beneath the flap and slowly opened the envelope. She stared at the bold title of the document and her heart shattered. A divorce decree. Aaron's signature was scrawled across the bottom. There was a yellow tab with an ugly red arrow pointing to the blank line with her name typed below it. All she had to do was sign it and her sham of a marriage would be over. Aaron Brody would be out of her life.

Tears ran down her cheeks and the print blurred as she twisted the simple band Aaron had placed on her finger. That simple. Sign her name.

There was a tap at the door and Edward stuck his head around, but didn't wait for her to invite him in. She grabbed a couple of tissues and blotted her face.

He took a seat in front of the desk as if it were any other day. "I've made a decision."

She flipped the decree facedown on her desk and refused to look at him. She didn't want Edward of all people to see her so vulnerable. "About what?"

Edward slid the papers out from beneath her trembling fingers and turned them over. She didn't say a word, just waited for him to gloat. She kept waiting. Not a sound. When she couldn't take another second, she glanced up to find him staring at her.

"I'm sorry," he said.

The tight knot in her throat choked any words. Instead, she shrugged and focused on the window, but she couldn't have said whether the sun was shining or not.

"This confirms my decision. I'm sending you home. Perry can finish getting the resort in shape to go on the market. The way the tourist industry down here is exploding, we should make a sizeable profit."

She took a deep breath. "We have to talk about Perry."

"One thing at a time. You need a year off. Go to Europe, get on top of this."

"A year off would give me too much time to think." She

sucked in a quick breath that came out more like a hiccup. Her own stupidity had finally done it, completely and irreversibly destroyed the one good thing in her life, her marriage. "I don't know how to take time off. All I know is work."

Edward came around the desk and pulled her into his arms. "I've scheduled a mover to come to the bungalow tomorrow. They'll take care of your furniture and car. You have a plane ticket to Boston for the day after. You can stay at the house and we'll figure out what to do." He pushed the hair out of her face. "You and Don are all I've got."

She backed away far enough to see his face. "Why didn't you tell me about your heart condition?"

"I…" Edward thrust one hand through his gray hair and let out a deep sigh. "How did you find out?"

"That's not important." She softened her tone. "Why didn't you let me be there for you?"

He recovered his composure. "It's not that serious."

Charlotte knew better. "It's serious enough that you suddenly wanted me in Boston learning the business. And you wanted me married and taken care of, not that I need to be taken care of, except in your mind."

"Of course I want the business to succeed." He dropped down into the wing chair and rubbed his palms down his thighs. "I need to know you and Don will always be taken care of financially. Your brother doesn't have the business sense to run his own affairs, much less Harrington's."

"And I'm a woman." She fed him the ammunition, praying she was wrong.

"Charlotte, you don't understand the dynamics of big business. Your knowledge and experience won't hold up when men play hardball." Edward glanced at the divorce papers. "I'm not saying this to hurt you, to Aaron the marriage was all about money. And without a prenuptial, he could take you for a cleaning. You didn't see it because you loved him."

She closed her eyes then opened them to look at Edward. "I need to be alone."

"I hate to see you hurting like this." He slowly stood and patted her shoulder.

Charlotte couldn't meet his eyes. She shook her head and stared out the window until she heard the door close.

She sniffed and blotted her nose with a tissue. With the best education money could buy and all her experience, was she still not smart enough to succeed in her field? Or her life?

She wiped her eyes. She'd worked her ass off to make this resort into a well-run, profitable business. No one, not Perry, or Edward, or her own latent insecurities were going to keep her from making sure Perry Thurman didn't screw her over a second time. Maybe it was too late to save her marriage, but Perry Thurman's career with Harrington's was about to take a nosedive.

She picked up the phone and dialed Monte Carlo for the fifth time this week only to get the same response. "Henri Broussard is on holiday." The man was avoiding her calls, but other than fly to France, she wasn't sure what to do about it. She'd even tried to ask for him in French, but her accent wasn't that good.

French? French! She grabbed her cell phone and headed for the restaurant. "Pierre, I need to see you a minute."

She used her cell and dialed the Monte Carlo number again and had Pierre ask for Monsieur Broussard. Within thirty seconds, he had the guy on the phone.

Charlotte took the receiver. "Henri, this is Charlotte Harrington."

AARON WALKED INTO THE GECKO and found Rosa sitting at the bar. She patted the stool next to her. "You doing okay?"

"Just peachy," he said, hoping she'd move on to some

mundane subject and not torture him with talk about the resort or his marriage.

Maybe he should move his boat to Cozumel or Belize.

"I'm looking for another job. I'm not working for that weasel, Thurman," Rosa said.

"What are you talking about?"

"With your wife moving back to Boston, Thurman's the new manager."

"The old man's sick. He needs Charlie at Harrington's head office," Aaron said.

"I heard she's flying home to Boston tomorrow, then taking some time off. She looks beat. Rumor is the resort's going on the market. So who knows if I'll even have a job." Rosa swirled her wine and watched Raul put clean glasses on the shelf. "Think that old ogre would fire his own granddaughter?"

Tomorrow? Aaron slammed his glass down. "Maybe, but not before he hears what I have to say."

He barged into Charlie's office and found old man Harrington going through her desk. "Where's Charlie?"

"Packing. The Keys haven't exactly been a pleasant experience for my granddaughter."

"You're a fool."

Harrington glared at him. "Look, Mr. Brody, she doesn't belong with you. Your marriage was a farce. It's finished. Charlotte is coming home and Perry's taking over here."

Aaron braced his hands on the desk and leaned into Harrington's face. "Charlie has worked her ass off the last five years to turn this place into the most elite resort on Marathon. Your reward for that kind of commitment is to replace her with that egotistical jackass who only wants to marry her so he can steal the company you spent your life building? Thurman doesn't have a tenth of your granddaughter's skill. He hasn't lifted a bloody finger to do anything except spy on us and cause chaos."

"He was put here to keep an eye on you and on the resort. I knew you were up to no good the minute Charlotte announced that ridiculous engagement."

"You're blind, Harrington. Charlie's not only the classiest woman I've ever met, she's the smartest person you could find to run this resort, or the whole damn Harrington empire for that matter." As he said the words, the reality of what he was giving up began to sink in. Maybe he was the biggest fool of all for letting Charlie go.

"I knew this marriage was a scam the first minute I laid eyes on you. Be a gentleman and walk away."

Aaron fought the urge to wrap his fingers around the old man's neck and forced his voice to stay low. "My marriage may have started out as a farce, but it's the best thing that ever happened in my whole screwed up life." He took a white envelope out of his pocket and held it up. "This is for Charlie. It should make us square on the hundred grand."

Harrington shrugged. "Keep the money. It's worth it to me to have you out of her life. Charlotte is going back to Boston with me."

"Charlotte makes her own decisions," Charlie said from the doorway.

Aaron turned and watched her approach, her eyes never wavering as they held him captive.

"And you know what, Edward?" she continued, without breaking eye contact with Aaron. "This is your resort and if you think it's in your best interest to have Perry run it, you deserve him. If you want to sell it, that's fine, too. But I'm not coming back to Boston with you. There are other jobs."

Aaron returned her stare. She hadn't looked away the whole time she was calmly telling old man Harrington where he could stick his business.

"Did you mean what you said, Aaron? Was marrying me the best thing you ever did?"

"Oh, yeah." He recognized her need for reassurance. He

ran one finger down her nose. "You're an amazing woman, Charlie Brody."

She beamed at Aaron, then turned back to her grandfather. "I'm going to stay in Marathon and prove to my husband how much I love him. I'm not giving up on this marriage."

"You love this low-class delinquent?"

Admiration showed in her smile. "There's nothing low-class about my husband. Aaron did all he could to save his mother and survive. I seriously doubt your son would've stolen to put food in your mouth if you were dying. We could both learn a few things about loyalty from Aaron. His friends would fight to the ends of the earth for him." She raised one eyebrow. "So would I."

Perry came through the open door in time to hear her last remarks. "You can't be serious about spending the rest of your life with a drug dealer."

Before Aaron could respond, Charlie jumped to his defense. "My husband doesn't have anything to do with drugs."

"I have proo—"

She didn't wait for him to finish. "If you had proof, you'd have run straight to the police."

Aaron turned to Charlie. "I think he's referring to the video-tape the police have of him planting cocaine on my boat."

He had the pleasure of a few seconds of speechlessness before Perry found his voice. "Why would I need to plant drugs on a known drug runner's boat?"

"Don't know. Should be interesting to see how you explain it in court."

"Maybe you'd like to explain this, while you're at it." Charlie handed Perry a stack of papers. "By my calculations, we're about eighteen thousand short."

"What?" Perry asked, not looking at the paper.

"Since you took over the financials the numbers look a little odd. Did you think I wouldn't notice?"

Edward grabbed the report out of Perry's hand and put his glasses on. "These don't add up." He focused on Perry. "Why? You don't need the money."

Charlotte wasn't done. "It wasn't about Perry wanting the money for himself, Grandfather. It was about Perry making it appear the resort was losing money under my management. And he was sending the money to Monte Carlo to pay off Henri Broussard to keep quiet about his little indiscretion with one of our top client's wives long enough to marry me and take control of Harrington's."

Both Edward and Perry were giving Charlie their undivided attention. Aaron couldn't tell who looked the most stunned.

Edward's jaw turned to steel. "It was all an act. Sitting by my bedside in Monte Carlo and pouring out your dreams for Harrington's and lamenting about how you worshiped my granddaughter. It was bullshit. All to serve your own selfish purpose. I trusted you."

"Her accusations are ridiculous. She's just trying to cover for her own incompetence," Perry insisted.

Charlie's beautiful brow furrowed. "Since you mentioned it, there is one more thing that doesn't add up. See, I kept trying to figure out why you would suddenly want to marry a woman you'd described as, quote, 'about as sexy as a telephone pole.' I mean it's not like back in college when you only wanted your foot in the door at Harrington's. You're already in. A girl has to wonder, you know. But according to Henri…" She paused.

Aaron glanced at Thurman. The guy squirmed as if he might wet his pants.

"There was this dignitary staying at the Monte Carlo resort." She cocked her head. "The rumor goes, Perry made a show of stopping by the man's table where he was entertaining another gentleman over lunch. It gets fuzzy about here, but the next thing I hear—"

"None of this is true." Thurman tugged at his tie and un-buttoned the top button of his shirt. "You can't prove anything."

"Oh, but I can." Charlie continued. "The story goes that the dignitary walked into his suite some half hour later, and his wife wasn't alone." Charlie focused on Thurman. "When hotel security ushered you out, your pants were still down around your ankles. That's on the security tape." She frowned. "Then after you learned of Edward's heart attack, you bribed Henri with the promise of a very lucrative bonus if he kept quiet long enough for you to take over Harrington's."

Thurman turned purple.

Edward raised both eyebrows and paled.

Charlotte's expression was as sweet as candy. "You were afraid that if you weren't part of the family when Edward found out about your little indiscretion, you'd be unemployed. By the way, Edward, I'd have the Monte Carlo books audited." Charlie handed Harrington a folder. "This is a log for the legal department. It's all there."

"Impressive." Aaron leaned over and kissed Charlie's cheek, then handed her the envelope. "We're even."

She opened the envelope and stared at the hundred thousand dollar check, before slowly ripping it in half. "That's the smartest investment I've ever made."

As much as he wanted to grab hold and hang on for eternity, he knew better. "You don't know what you're saying. My life might sound romantic, but I can't picture you living hand to mouth and sleeping on a boat."

Charlie wrapped her arms around his neck. "I love sleeping with you on that boat. But, Aaron, I have money of my own. Although I'm not as rich as Edward, we aren't destitute. Your business is doing well. I can find another job. We'll be fine." She offered her mouth up to his. "I love you."

He cupped her gorgeous face in his hands. Afraid to close

his eyes, for fear she might disappear, he searched the depths of her coffee-brown eyes. "I love you, too, Charlie Brody."

"But, you can't stay married to this nobody," Perry sputtered.

Harrington turned to Charlie. "Charlotte, you are all I have. I need you in Boston. Think very hard about what you're doing here."

She placed her hand in Aaron's. "It's all I've thought about for days." She turned to Edward. "If you're really interested in my help, we can discuss it. I have some workable ideas."

She and Aaron headed toward the door just as Officer Perez entered.

Aaron took a tiny tape recorder out of his pocket and handed it to him. "Thanks for your help. I owe you."

Charlotte's heart raced as she squeezed Aaron's hand. As they made the journey across the resort to the wharf, she couldn't stop smiling.

She glanced at the *Free Wind* and squealed as Aaron scooped her up into his arms. "What's this?"

"Man's supposed to carry his bride over the threshold." He raised both eyebrows in a gesture that insinuated he had no intention of putting her down until they reached the little berth below deck.

"Looks like a gangplank to me," she corrected.

"Minor detail, sweetheart."

She buried her face in the crook of his neck and giggled.

"What's so funny?"

"I love being in your arms. I had no idea I could feel this free, this happy."

"You just told your grandfather to take the resort and stick it where the sun don't shine. We may starve in each other's arms."

"We won't starve." She nibbled his ear and ran her tongue around the inside curve.

Aaron Brody loved her. He honest to God loved her.

* * * * *

*Celebrate 60 years of pure
reading pleasure with Harlequin!*

To commemorate the event, Harlequin Intrigue® is
thrilled to invite you to the wedding of The Colby
Agency's J. T. Baxley and his bride, Eve Mattson.

That is, of course, if J.T. can find the woman who left
him at the altar. Considering he's a private investigator
for one of the top agencies in the country—the best of
the best—that shouldn't be a problem. The real setback
is that his bride isn't who she appears to be…and her
mysterious past has put them both in danger.

*Enjoy an exclusive glimpse
of Debra Webb's latest addition to*
THE COLBY AGENCY:
ELITE RECONNAISSANCE DIVISION

THE BRIDE'S SECRETS

Available August 2009 from Harlequin Intrigue®.

The dark figures on the dock were still firing. The bullets cutting through the surface of the water without the warning boom of shots told Eve they were using silencers.

That was to her benefit. Silencers decreased the accuracy of every shot and lessened the range.

She grabbed for the rocks. Scrambled through the darkness. Bumped her knee on a boulder. Cursed.

Burrowing into the waist-deep grass, she kept low and crawled forward. Faster. Pushed harder. Needed as much distance as possible.

Shots pinged on the rocks.

J.T. scrambled alongside her.

He was breathing hard.

They had to stay close to the ground until they reached the next row of warehouses. Even though she was relatively certain they were out of range at this point, she wasn't taking any risks. And she wasn't slowing down.

J.T. had to keep up.

The splat of a bullet hitting the ground next to Eve had her rolling left. Maybe they weren't completely out of range.

She bumped J.T. He grunted.

His injured arm. Dammit. She could apologize later.

Half a dozen more yards.

Almost in the clear.

As she reached the cover of the alley between the first two warehouses she tensed.

Silence.

No pings or splats.

She glanced back at the dock. Deserted.

Time to run.

Her car was parked another block down.

Pushing to her feet, she sprinted forward. The wet bag dragged at her shoulder. She ignored it.

By the time she reached the lot where her car was parked, she had dug the keys from her pocket and hit the fob. Six seconds later she was behind the wheel. She hit the ignition as J.T. collapsed into the passenger seat. Tires squealed as she spun out of the slot.

"What the hell did you do to me?"

From the corner of her eye she watched him shake his head in an attempt to clear it.

He would be pissed when she told him about the tranquilizer.

She'd needed him cooperative until she formulated a plan. A drug-induced state of unconsciousness had been the fastest and most efficient method to ensure his continued solidarity.

"I can't really talk right now." Eve weaved into the right lane as the street widened to four lanes. What she needed was traffic. It was Saturday night—shouldn't be that difficult to find as soon as they were out of the old warehouse district.

A glance in the rearview mirror warned that their unwanted company had caught up.

Sensing her tension, J.T. turned to peer over his left shoulder.

"I hope you have a plan B."

She shot him a look. "There's always plan G." Then she pulled the Glock out of her waistband.

Cutting the steering wheel left, she slid between two vehicles. Another veer to the right and she'd put several cars between hers and the enemy.

She was betting they wouldn't pull out the firepower in the open like this, but a girl could never be too sure when it came to an unknown enemy.

Deep blending was the way to go.

Two traffic lights ahead the marquis of a movie theater provided exactly the opportunity she was looking for.

The digital numbers on the dash indicated it was just past midnight. Perfect timing. The late movie would be purging its audience into the crowd of teenagers who liked hanging out in the parking lot.

She took a hard right onto the property that sported a twelve-screen theater, numerous fast-food hot spots and a chain superstore. Speeding across the lot, she selected a lane of parking slots. Pulling in as close to the theater entrance as possible, she shut off the engine and reached for her door.

"Let's go."

Thankfully he didn't argue.

Rounding the hood of her car, she shoved the Glock into her bag, then wrapped her arm around J.T.'s and merged into the crowd.

With her free hand she finger-combed her long hair. It was soaked, as were her clothes. The kids she bumped into noticed, gave her death-ray glares.

They just didn't know.

As she and J.T. moved in closer to the building, she grabbed a baseball cap from an innocent bystander. The crowd made it easy. The kid who owned the cap had made it even easier by stuffing the cap bill-first into his waistband at the small of his back.

Pushing through the loitering crowd, she made her way to the side of the building next to the main entrance. She pushed

J.T. against the wall and dropped her bag to the ground. Peeled off her tee and let it fall.

His gaze instantly zeroed in on her breasts, where the cami she wore had glued to her skin like an extra layer. A zing of desire shot through her veins.

Not the time.

With a flick of her wrist she twisted her hair up and clamped the cap atop the blonde mass.

"They're coming," J.T. muttered as he gazed at some point beyond her.

"Yeah, I know." She planted her palms against the wall on either side of him and leaned in. "Keep your eyes open. Let me know when they're inside."

Then she planted her lips on his.

* * * * *

Will J.T. and Eve be caught in the moment?
Or will Eve get the chance to reveal all of her secrets?
Find out in
THE BRIDE'S SECRETS
by Debra Webb
Available August 2009 from Harlequin Intrigue®

We'll be spotlighting a different series every month
throughout 2009 to celebrate our 60th anniversary.

LOOK FOR
HARLEQUIN INTRIGUE®
IN AUGUST!

To commemorate the event, Harlequin Intrigue® is thrilled
to invite you to the wedding of the Colby Agency's
J. T. Baxley and his bride, Eve Mattson.

Look for *Colby Agency: Elite Reconnaissance*

THE BRIDE'S SECRETS
BY DEBRA WEBB

Available August 2009

www.eHarlequin.com

HIBPA09

REQUEST YOUR FREE BOOKS!

2 FREE NOVELS PLUS 2
FREE GIFTS!

⟩*American ★ Romance*®

Love, Home & Happiness!

You're invited to join our Tell Harlequin Reader Panel!

By joining our new reader panel you will:

- Receive Harlequin® books—they are FREE and yours to keep with no obligation to purchase anything!
- Participate in fun online surveys
- Exchange opinions and ideas with women just like you
- Have a say in our new book ideas and help us publish the best in women's fiction

In addition, you will have a chance to win great prizes and receive special gifts!
See Web site for details. Some conditions apply.
Space is limited.

To join, visit us at
www.TellHarlequin.com.

HRI7601

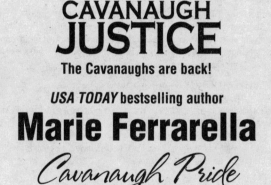

CAVANAUGH
JUSTICE

The Cavanaughs are back!

USA TODAY bestselling author
Marie Ferrarella

Cavanaugh Pride

In charge of searching for a serial killer on the loose, Detective Frank McIntyre has his hands full. When Detective Julianne White Bear arrives in town searching for her missing cousin, Frank has to keep the escalating danger under control while trying to deny the very real attraction he has for Julianne. Can they keep their growing feelings under wraps while also handling the most dangerous case of their careers?

Available August wherever books are sold.

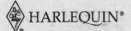

HARLEQUIN®

American ★ Romance®

COMING NEXT MONTH
Available August 11, 2009

#1269 THE RODEO RIDER by Roxann Delaney
Men Made in America
A vacation was all attorney Jules Vandeveer needed to clear her head. But rest was the last thing on her mind when she met rodeo rider Tanner O'Brien. Jules was immediately drawn to the rugged cowboy, and her heart went out to him and his rebellious nephew. Helping them heal wasn't a problem...but for once, walking away would be.

#1270 MISTLETOE MOMMY by Tanya Michaels
4 Seasons in Mistletoe
Dr. Adam Varner planned this trip to Mistletoe to reconnect with his kids. When he rescued a stranded pet sitter with car trouble, he didn't expect Brenna Pierce to have such an amazing connection with his daughters and son. Brenna is the woman Adam didn't know he was looking for—can he make a temporary stay in Mistletoe into something more...permanent?

#1271 SAMANTHA'S COWBOY by Marin Thomas
Samantha Cartwright needs to access her trust fund to start up a ranch for abused horses. Wade Dawson needs to keep Samantha distracted until he can figure out where her missing money went! So Wade spends as much time at Sam's ranch as he can—and, with Sam, discovers his inner cowboy....

#1272 ONE OF A KIND DAD by Daly Thompson
Fatherhood
Daniel Foster has built his own family looking after foster kids. And when he meets Lilah Ross and starts to fall for her, he knows he wants Lilah and her young son to be a part of that family, too. But when Lilah's ex-husband threatens her son, Daniel is afraid he could lose them both.

www.eHarlequin.com

HARCNMBPA0709